ICE CREAM AND
SWEET DREAMS

ICE CREAM AND
SWEET DREAMS

Coco Simon

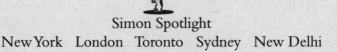

Simon Spotlight

New York   London   Toronto   Sydney   New Delhi

SIMON SPOTLIGHT
An imprint of Simon & Schuster Children's Publishing Division
1230 Avenue of the Americas, New York, New York 10020
This Simon Spotlight edition December 2020
Copyright © 2020 by Simon & Schuster, Inc.
All rights reserved, including the right of reproduction in whole or in part in any form.
SIMON SPOTLIGHT and colophon are registered trademarks of Simon & Schuster, Inc.
For information about special discounts for bulk purchases, please contact
Simon & Schuster Special Sales at 1-866-506-1949 or business@simonandschuster.com.
Text by Caroline Smith Hickey
Cover illustrations by Alisa Coburn
Cover design by Alisa Coburn and Hannah Frece
Interior design by Hannah Frece
The text of this book was set in Bembo Std.
Manufactured in the United States of America 1020 OFF
10 9 8 7 6 5 4 3 2 1
ISBN 978-1-5344-8080-3 (pbk)
ISBN 978-1-5344-8081-0 (hc)
ISBN 978-1-5344-8082-7 (eBook)
Library of Congress Catalog Card Number 2020943564

CHAPTER ONE

BRAIN FREEZE

It was one of those surprisingly cold days in spring that made you realize winter still wasn't completely over yet. I stared out the window of Molly's Ice Cream shop, where I was working my regular Sunday shift with my two best friends, Allie Shear and Tamiko Sato. I pictured pulling my favorite sunny yellow sweater out of storage and putting on fuzzy socks when I got home later.

The town of Bayville was a beachside town, which meant that we usually had a steady stream of ice cream lovers coming through the shop. But on days like today, when the thermometer dipped below 50 degrees and the wind was blowing, people had their minds on other things.

"Earth to Sierra. Are you in there?" Allie teased, waving a hand in front of my face.

"She's probably writing song lyrics in her head," said Tamiko, who was holding chalk and an eraser, and staring up at the shop's two giant chalkboards. One was for the daily special—something our social marketing and flavor genius, Tamiko, was excellent at dreaming up—and one was for Allie's ice cream and book pairings, where our bookworm, Allie, appealed to the book lovers in town by matching a classic read with just the right treat.

But today both boards had been wiped bare, and Tamiko stood staring at the wall, as if she didn't have a single idea.

"No lyrics in this head!" I replied. "At least not today. Anyway, Tessa writes most of our song lyrics. She's the one with all the inspiration."

Tessa was one of my bandmates in my rock band, the Wildflowers. And while we did write and perform our own music, I was the lead singer and left most of the songwriting up to everyone else.

"Maybe you should call her," Tamiko suggested. "Because, girl, we need some inspiration *here. Now.*

This place is dead! We need an amazing, fresh spring flavor to bring people in."

"You're right, Tamiko," Sierra said. "We have a reputation for more than just delicious homemade ice cream. It's our originality that keeps people coming back."

"Agreed," said Allie. "My mom can make anything work! Look how well all of the new dairy-free flavors have done."

Thanks to some "inspiration" from Tamiko's brother, Kai, Molly's had recently started carrying one or two dairy-free flavors. I couldn't believe how good they were—and made entirely with coconut milk!

"So then, *where* can we go for inspiration around here?" Tamiko wondered aloud.

"We went to the boardwalk a few times," Allie replied. "It was fun, but I don't think we'll find any new inspiration there."

"Maybe you should call Colin and ask him for some ideas," I said, nudging Allie with my shoulder.

Allie had recently been spending a lot of time studying at the library with Colin, her longtime crush and her closest friend at Vista Green.

"Why would I ask Colin?" Allie asked, blushing furiously and wiping at an imaginary spot on the clean countertops. "I doubt he knows anything about ice cream flavors."

Just then Allie's mother appeared from the little office at the back of the shop, which we all called "backstage."

"It's awfully quiet out here, girls. What's going on? No crazy new flavor ideas, Tamiko? No book pairings, Allie? Sierra can't pour on her charm if there are no customers in here!"

I loved when Mrs. Shear said I was charming. Being charming wasn't something I did consciously. I just happened to have a very outgoing personality and really liked people. When I was around a crowd, I lit up and felt naturally cheerful. What can I say? I'm a people person!

"No new pairings or specials yet," Allie said. "It's cold outside, and our brains are tired from all of our homework and eighth-grade responsibilities. We need something exciting to get our creative juices flowing!"

Mrs. Shear pulled something from her back pocket and laid it down on the counter in front of us. It was a brochure for Peg and Mary's Ice Cream Museum and Factory.

"An ice cream *museum*?" Tamiko squealed. "How have I never heard of this before?"

"It sounds amazing!" I said. "Can you imagine the toppings they must have? And different types of cones?"

"And all the old equipment and hand cranks?" Allie added.

Mrs. Shear beamed. "I thought you girls would be interested. What do you think about the Sprinkle Sundays sisters going on a little 'research' field trip with me next week? Maybe on Tuesday? I can check with your parents and make sure it's okay."

We didn't waste a second. All three of us screamed at once, "Yes!"

The only thing more fun than a field trip with your two best friends was a field trip to *an ice cream factory* with your two best friends.

"Do they have samples?" Allie asked. "They must have *samples*, right?"

Mrs. Shear nodded. "Oh yes, indeed. They have a movie about the old days of making ice cream, a production room, and even a 'Flavoroom.' I think this is just the thing we need to gear up for spring! When you have a year-round business based on a summer staple, you need to always be prepared to think big. Now, girls, put some music on, brainstorm, and see what you can come up with for today!"

Mrs. Shear left the brochure for us to look at and went backstage again to deal with whatever office work had piled up.

Tamiko browsed the brochure, while I put on an upbeat song from my current favorite playlist on my phone.

Allie stared and stared at the chalkboard before finally saying, "What do you guys think of pairing *Alice's Adventures in Wonderland* by Lewis Carroll with our Tea and Crumpets flavor? After all, the Mad Hatter tea party scene is pretty famous, and tea is a good drink for a cool spring day. . . ."

"I love it!" I said, clapping my hands. Allie always came up with the best ideas for book pairings.

Tamiko shook her head sadly. "You're doing your job, Alley Cat. If only I could do mine. My mind has just been blank lately! I promise—I'm going to do better, or my name isn't 'Tamiko Sato'!"

I wrapped my arm around Tamiko's shoulder and

gave her a squeeze. "Knowing you, you'll have five fabulous new ideas before tomorrow. Don't worry. We're a team! And we've got our factory tour to look forward to. We'll get tons of new ideas!"

Tamiko nodded, but I could tell she still felt bad. Recently Tamiko had gone through a bit of a braggy phase, thinking she was the queen of just about everything—art, schoolwork, our jobs at Molly's. She'd ended up hurting her brother in the process, and since then she had been more subdued than usual. I was ready for the old outrageous and out-landish (but not braggy!) Tamiko to make her return.

"We're going to come up with something new and fabulous, or we're not the Sprinkle Sundays sis-ters," I said. I wrapped my other arm around Allie and pulled them both to me. "Get ready for greatness!"

CHAPTER TWO

WHO'S A STAR?

After work I walked home, enjoying the chill in the air and wondering what delicious food my father might be making for dinner. My parents were both veterinarians and ran their own veterinary clinic. They often worked long hours during the week, so they always made sure to have a big family dinner on Sunday evenings, and usually my father was the chef. Both of my parents had been born in Cuba, and my father liked nothing better than to spend an afternoon cooking up one of his grandmother's favorite recipes for the family.

I was feeling so excited about the beautiful spring day and the ice cream museum field trip with my friends that I practically skipped up the steps to my front door. When I burst inside, I dropped my bag in the hallway and yelled out that I was home.

"Hola! Ya llegué!"

From upstairs my mother replied, *"Hola,* Sierra!" but from the kitchen I heard only a "Whoops! That was more than a pinch."

A *pinch*? A pinch of what?

I smelled something rich and slightly smoky cooking. I couldn't quite place it, which was unusual because my nose knew most of my father's signature dishes by heart. I headed toward the kitchen, but paused to pet my cat, Marshmallow, as she twined between my legs.

"What is that yummy smell, Papi?" I asked as I stepped into the kitchen. But to my surprise, my father wasn't there. It was my twin, Isa, standing in front of the big gas range, stirring an enormous pot of something. "Oh, hey. What are you doing?"

Isa flipped her bangs out of her face and rolled her eyes. She was practically an expert at both gestures. "I'm making *cocido de garbanzos*—chickpea stew."

I thought hard for a moment. I didn't remember ever having *cocido de garbanzos* before. "Is that one of Papi's dishes?"

Isa shook her head. "No. He got called in for an emergency—a schnauzer ate some raisins and needed his stomach pumped. And Mami is catching up on paperwork, so Papi told me I could be in charge of dinner. I went online, found a recipe, and went for it. I think I just overdid it on the paprika, though."

Isa shrugged, as if it didn't matter too much one way or the other. I had *not* inherited the cooking bug from our father, and my idea of making a snack was to grab a granola bar on my way from one activity to another. But Isa, who was my identical twin and yet pretty much my opposite in every single way, had begun to cook recently and was trying increasingly harder dishes.

I couldn't help being impressed. I had almost zero confidence in my kitchen skills (I didn't even scoop the ice cream at Molly's—I ran the cash register and handled most of the customer service issues!) and never would have tried to make a completely new recipe by myself without my father there to help me.

Isa was always willing to try something hard and risk failing. That was why she was the only girl on an all-boys travel soccer team. She'd had the guts to show up and try out for it. And once the coaches had seen how good she was, they'd had to take her. It was something I'd always admired about her.

"Will Papi be home in time to eat with us?" I asked.

Isa shook her head. "I don't think so. The food is ready now, and he said not to wait for him in case they have to keep the schnauzer for observation for a few hours."

"How did the owners not know that raisins are poisonous to dogs?" I wondered aloud. "We've never even *had* a dog, and we know that. Raisins, grapes, avocados, gum with xylitol, chocolate. They're all bad for dogs."

Isa laughed. "I know, right? But I guess everyone can't be the daughters of two veterinarians. We've grown up listening to all the things our parents have had to fix for other people's pets, so it makes sense that we'd know it."

Something about the way Isa had grouped us together, as "the daughters of two veterinarians," made me feel strangely warm inside. Normally Isa tried to pretend that we *weren't* identical twins. She wore black almost exclusively, while I wore bright colors, textured tights, and fun leggings. She'd had her hair cut into a fauxhawk a year ago and dyed the tips purple, while I left mine long and curly and naturally brown. It was nice to hear her mention us being the same in some ways.

"Your stew smells great," I told her. "It's the perfect thing to eat on this chilly spring day!"

Isa beamed, clearly pleased by my compliment. "That's exactly why I picked it," she said. "Cold weather means soup!"

"I'll set the table," I offered, "since you did all the cooking. And I'll tell Mami to come and eat with us."

The stew turned out to be delicious, and while our Sunday dinner wasn't as festive as it usually was, because my dad was gone, the meal was still pretty nice. For a moment I felt a pang for my friend Allie, whose parents had divorced more than a year before. She now split her time between her mom's house and her dad's apartment. She'd even had to transfer schools at the start of seventh grade, which meant that she no longer was at school with me and Tamiko. Her parents did a great job of keeping things friendly, and they even had dinner together, all four of them— Allie, her mom, her dad, and sometimes her brother, Tanner. But I wondered what it would be like in my house to not have our regular Sunday family dinners.

I unexpectedly volunteered to do all the dishes myself, even though I absolutely hated cleaning up. My parents did too, which was why our house was usually a bit, well, untidy. But I did the dishes anyway, so that Mami could get back to her paperwork and because Isa had obviously worked hard to make our dinner. She cheered when I offered and practically ran to escape up to her room.

By the time I'd finished the dishes and wiped all the counters, I was enjoying the lingering warmth and smell of the kitchen so much that I decided to do my homework there, even though I normally preferred the privacy of my bedroom.

I wanted to make sure I saw Papi went he got home, and I wanted to also remind myself how lucky I was to have my family together, all in one house. Maybe we weren't perfect all the time, but we were there for one another.

I gathered my books and spread out at the kitchen table. I started on my geometry homework first. Even though I was usually a whiz at math, geometry was taking some time for me to get used to. Rays, planes, complementary and supplementary angles . . . it was like a new language. I loved computing numbers in my head. In fact, I did it all the time working the register at Molly's. But geometry was a totally different kind of math.

To my surprise, after I'd been working for about a half hour, Isa came back downstairs and plopped down in the chair across from me.

She was nibbling on a dark chocolate bar. It must have been stashed up in her room. If Isa had a weakness, it was dark chocolate.

She sat quietly for a minute or two, just watching me work on problem number fifteen. This was not how things normally went in our house. Isa did not *linger* around any of us—she liked to be alone. Something had to be up.

"What's up?" I said finally.

She shrugged innocently. "Why should something be up?" she asked.

I gave her the I-know-my-twin-sister face and raised an eyebrow. "Since when do you enjoy watching me try to figure out the degree of an angle?"

"It's thirty-seven degrees," she said. "You've got to subtract fifty-three from ninety, because *that* one is a right angle. You can tell by the little square mark there, and that's how you know they total ninety."

I looked back down at my paper and saw that she was right. I hurriedly did the equation on my homework sheet so that my teacher could see how I'd gotten the answer.

"Thanks," I said.

"No big deal." Another minute or two passed, and then Isa said, "So, what's new with you, rock star? Do the Wildflowers have any gigs coming up? I haven't heard you practicing as much."

This conversation was almost unprecedented. Isa cared about my *band*? She had come to a few of our performances, but she almost never asked me—randomly—how things were going with the group.

"Um, well, we've been practicing, but I guess not quite as much lately. Everyone's had so much schoolwork. Plus, we don't have a gig coming up right now. But I'm sure we'll get back into our groove soon."

"Would you say your voice is in good shape?" she prodded.

I put my pencil down. "Excuse me, *what*? Why are you asking me all this stuff?"

Isa opened her eyes wide, playing innocent. "Can't I take an interest in my dear, sweet twin sister?"

I narrowed my own eyes. Something was up. Something was *definitely* up. "Spill it, Isa. You're acting weird, maybe even more weird than when you snuck a *snake* into the house last year and told me that your grand plan to hide it from Mami and Papi was to keep it in your closet forever."

Isa laughed. "Not one of my best ideas."

I laughed too, in spite of myself. I couldn't help it. Seeing Isa happy made me happy. "Just tell me whatever is going on with you, so I can finish my homework."

"Okay, okay." She pulled a folded piece of paper from the front pocket of her hoodie and handed it to me. The paper felt soft, and the creases were slightly worn, as if it had been folded and unfolded many times.

I opened it. It was an ad.

It's time to find the
NEXT YOUNG SINGING
SENSATION!
Could it be YOU?
Come and audition for the
WHO'S A STAR? singing contest!

*If you're selected as a finalist, you will
appear on our local TV station,
where fans will decide our big winner!*

I read over the flyer twice, soaking in the information. I had heard of Who's a Star? They traveled around to different cities, holding local singing contests for teenagers. The judges were real music producers, and the winner of the contest got a free, exclusive tour of the music recording studios in Los Angeles and would sing a song on an upcoming holiday special on national TV.

"What do you think?" asked Isa. "I saw the flyer posted on the bulletin board outside the grocery store earlier, and I thought you should do it."

I felt a series of tingles all over my body. I was nervous, excited, scared, hopeful, and anxious. A singing contest? It was like a dream come true!

"When is it?" I asked, my eyes scanning the tiny type at the bottom of the page.

"It's the end of next week."

"Next *week*? Isa, I can't be ready by then. What will I sing? Am I even good enough to try out?" I blubbered.

Isa raised her eyebrows. "There's only one way to find out, right?"

I nodded, trying to take deep breaths. I could feel something like hope blooming in my stomach. I knew I couldn't get ready for the audition by myself, though—I'd need my band to help prepare me. And of course I needed Allie and Tamiko to tell me if I could even do it!

I wanted to call them all immediately. But I also wanted to tell them in person. And maybe think about it overnight . . . just in case. Just in case I wasn't sure I was brave enough to audition in front of real talent professionals and other kids who'd surely been singing much longer than I had. After all, I'd just started with my band last year. I hadn't had any formal training or anything!

I was sunny Sierra. I was charming and outgoing. I was good at juggling lots of things, and I tried to be a good friend to my Sprinkle Sundays sisters. But was I a star? I didn't know. But it seemed like there was a way to find out.

CHAPTER THREE

THE REAL DEAL

When I walked into school Monday morning, I immediately set out to find Tamiko and MacKenzie, one of my other close friends at school. I was bursting at the seams to tell them my news. I wished for the millionth time that Allie was still at MLK Middle School with us, and not living it up over at Vista Green, which was a recently renovated school with amazing cafeteria food and new, functioning lockers. Who needed good food when you had your besties with you?

I finally found Tamiko outside the science lab wing, asking for notes for a lab she'd missed. She was wearing her favorite purple-and-red minidress and a pair of black high-top sneakers, with her hair pulled into three skinny braids. She was always coming up with something new and different to wear to school.

"TAMIKO!" I yelled as I skidded to a stop in front of her. I'd been using my speed-walk, something I'd perfected after years of rushing from classes to student council meetings to soccer practices to band practices, etc. My speed-walk was almost a run, but more in control, and kept the teachers off my back about running in the halls.

Tamiko whirled around, looking alarmed, as if she were expecting me to yell "Fire!" or something. Whoops. Maybe I needed to tone it down.

"WHAT?" she yelled back.

I stood in front of her, bouncing on my toes. "I have to tell you something, but I want to tell Allie at the same time, and probably MacKenzie, too. How can I do that?"

I realized as I was talking that I was maybe, *possibly* making this whole audition thing a much bigger deal than it really was. Anyone up to eighteen years old could try out. There would be tons of talented, older, more experienced singers there at Who's a Star? Why did I think this was worth getting so amped about? Did I really think I had a shot?

Either Tamiko was able to read my face or she just knows me really well, because she said, "There *is* a way for you to tell us all at the same time—at lunch! I'll text Allie and let her know we're going to video-chat with her while we eat. Okay?"

I bounced a few more times. "Okay. I reallllllllly want to tell you now, though."

Tamiko grinned and leaned in closer. "Go ahead, then. . . . Tell me."

"No! I'm going to wait. I think. Yes! At lunch! I've got to run to social studies because Mrs. Saunders hinted on Friday that we might have a pop quiz this morning."

"Oh, fine. Go study." Tamiko whipped out her phone and texted Allie. "I'll be ready for your news at lunch! I can't wait!"

To my surprise, the morning flew by. I was actually grateful for the fact that I had some of my harder classes on Monday mornings, because it kept my mind busy, when all I wanted to do was space out and think about the Who's a Star? contest.

At lunch I found Tamiko and MacKenzie already waiting for me at our usual table. MacKenzie looked up and waved as I made my way over to the table, and it was obvious Tamiko had filled her in.

"That was the longest morning of my *life*," Tamiko said dramatically. "Don't ever do this to me again, Sierra Perez."

"I won't," I promised. "Anyway, I feel silly making a huge deal about this. I should have just called you all last night!"

MacKenzie nodded. She was wearing a wide green headband that contrasted beautifully with her long red hair, and she looked almost as anxious as Tamiko to hear my news.

"I'm getting Allie up for a video chat now....Hang on." Tamiko propped her phone up against a math textbook, and MacKenzie scooted around beside us so she could see the screen too. Allie's face popped up a minute later, surrounded by bookshelves.

"Allie, are you in the *library*?" asked Tamiko.

"Yes!" she whispered. "We're not allowed on our phones in the cafeteria anymore. I'm in the stacks. Shhh! Now tell me the news! Sierra, do the Wildflowers have a new gig somewhere?"

"Or did one of your songs get picked up on the radio?" guessed MacKenzie.

"Are you guys making a music video? I could help style you!" Tamiko offered. "Please let me style you."

At this point it was abundantly clear that I had oversold my news. But there was no choice but to plunge ahead.

"Nothing has happened . . . *yet*," I said. "But Isa saw this flyer yesterday for a contest over in Hamilton, and it's for teen singers, ages thirteen to eighteen. It's the Who's a Star? singing contest. If you make it past the first round of auditions and become a finalist, you can appear on TV!"

Even as I said it, I started to get more and more excited. I wanted to win. I really, really wanted to win.

Allie gasped, then immediately clapped her hand over her mouth. "Sierra!" she whispered loudly. "That is amazing! That contest sounds like it was *made* for you!"

Tamiko started applauding, and MacKenzie squealed and gave me a huge hug.

"This is awesome! It'll be so much fun! And now I can style you for your *audition*!" Tamiko shrieked.

I waved my hand at her, urging her to keep her

voice down. I didn't think I wanted everyone to know about it. What if I didn't do well? And everyone knew? They would all ask me about it the next day. It seemed like something I might want to keep just between me and my besties. And my band. And my family.

"You're such a great singer, Sierra," MacKenzie gushed. "And you have a lot of presence on stage when you sing. It's your charisma!"

"And her natural beauty and charm," Allie chimed in.

"And her natural sunshine," said Tamiko.

I could feel myself blushing. I knew I could count on my friends for some confidence-boosting and compliments! Normally I didn't need them so much. I usually felt very good about my schoolwork and activities and even myself. But this was different. It was the real deal. Singing in front of *judges*.

"Okay. Let's keep a lid on it for now, because I'm not sure I want everyone in the whole school to know, all right?"

All three of my friends nodded in agreement. "Totes," said Tamiko.

"On the down low," agreed MacKenzie.

Allie suddenly looked up, alarmed. "Guys," she whispered. "I'm about to get busted. But I'll talk to you all later tonight! Congrats, Sierra!"

"Don't congratulate me!" I said. "I haven't done anything yet."

Tamiko put her arm around me. "Greatness just follows some people around, Sierra. You can't help that you're naturally awesome."

The Wildflowers almost always practiced on Mondays, which gave me a great opportunity to tell them my news too. But I wanted to be a little more chill about this announcement. After all, my bandmates were musicians. They would understand immediately how stiff the competition would be at this contest. They'd know that I would be up against some very, very good singers.

Our band practiced at Reagan's house in her garage, which was all set up with a large space for the instruments, as well as an old couch, a rug, some lamps, and a mini-fridge. Reagan had red hair, and she was always wearing it in unusual ways. Today she had it slicked back into a high bun, and then had pulled and sculpted the bun itself to look like

SPRINKLE SUNDAYS

a shiny hair bow. It was really impressive.

Tessa sat tuning her guitar, while Reagan poured some pretzels and peanuts into bowls for everyone, and Kasey flipped through some sheet music. It was just like the start of every other practice, and it was so nice to NOT be thinking, worrying, or talking about the contest for a moment that I decided to wait until the end of our practice to tell them. That way I wouldn't be a distraction either.

We warmed up with a few of our favorites, including a song Tessa had written specifically for me a few months before, called "Stand Up, Speak Up." It was a reminder that being nice wasn't more important than remembering to stand up for yourself and your friends. I sang it at home all the time in the shower. It had become one of my personal anthems.

Practice went well, but not great. I was distracted, so I forgot the lyrics to a few songs that I knew really well, and Reagan seemed a bit off beat here and there. But overall it was fun, and we brainstormed some new ideas for songs.

When we'd finished, we all plopped down onto the couch and passed around the pretzel bowl. I had to go home for dinner shortly, but I was always starv-

26

ing after school, and singing made me hungry too.

I decided this would be a good time to make my announcement.

"So I think I'm going to try out for a local singing contest next week," I said casually. "It's in Hamilton. I have to prepare a song, and if the judges choose me as one of the ten finalists, I get to appear on TV."

Immediately Tessa, Reagan, and Kasey all jumped up and started talking at once.

"A contest?"

"Ten finalists?"

"You'll be on TV?"

Reagan grabbed my hand and held on, jumping up and down while holding it. "This is so great! You'll be the best. I know it!"

"And you'll look beautiful on TV," added Tessa. "You have such great curly hair."

I was quiet for a moment. Then I asked, "Do you guys really think I can do it?"

They all screamed at once, "YES!"

"We'll *make* you do it," said Kasey. "Just remember when you win to mention that you're in a band!"

"And that it's called 'the Wildflowers,'" said Reagan.

"I can't believe I know a celebrity," added Tessa teasingly. "You're going to do *great*."

I nodded, pleased that they were all excited for me. I hadn't quite expected them to react so optimistically. But my band knew what it meant to do something like this. It took a lot of guts!

"I just wish you'd told us at the start of practice today so we could have helped you rehearse!" said Reagan. "I've got a study group tonight for a project, so I can't practice any longer."

"And I have three tests tomorrow," said Kasey glumly.

"How about an extra practice this Wednesday?" Tessa asked. "To help Sierra get ready? We can have her perform different songs for us, pick which one works best, critique her performance . . ."

Critique. I wasn't sure I liked the sound of that. It was probably a smart idea, though.

"You just wait," said Reagan. "You're going to be so prepared, the judges won't believe it. You'll have talent agents and managers calling you."

Suddenly the small amount of nerves I'd had flapping around in my stomach started to creep up the back of my neck. This contest wasn't like band practice in Reagan's garage, or singing in someone's backyard for a group of kids hanging out together. Or recording songs and playing them for our friends.

This was real. It was PUBLIC. And it was going to be a little scary.

CHAPTER FOUR
SUNSHINE AND SECRETS

Normally my mom picked me up from band practice at Reagan's on Mondays, but today it was my dad who came.

I slid into the front seat beside him and gave him a kiss on the cheek. "*Hola*, Papi."

"*Hola*, Sierra," he replied. "How was practice?"

"Good! We're working on some new songs, which is fun because it means we're trying new things. It can be hard, though, because it takes us a while to get them to sound good!"

My dad nodded. "It is a beautiful thing to create music, Sierra."

I knew this was a good opportunity to tell him about the contest, but I wanted to tell him and my mom together. So I purposely changed the subject.

"How was everything at the clinic today?" I asked.

My dad shook his head. "Very busy. Some days it's *too* busy. Your mother and I wouldn't mind a quiet day now and then. But I guess it's good that so many people are taking care of their pets."

Not long ago my parents wouldn't even have thought of letting me and Isa have any pets at home, because they were so busy taking care of them at work all day! But then, luckily, a litter of kittens came our way, and my parents let us each keep one. Marshmallow and Cinnamon were like members of our family now.

"Wait, Papi! Stop. Pull over!" I pointed to the right. "There's Isa, walking home."

My dad pulled the car over. Isa was walking just ahead of us down the sidewalk, her back to us. She had her enormous headphones on, and she must have been listening to something she liked, because her head was bobbing back and forth as she walked.

"Isa!" I called out. *"Isa!"*

My dad honked the horn, and finally she turned around, scowling. When she recognized us, though, instead of smiling, she looked nervous.

She walked up to the car and climbed into the back seat. She did not look happy that we were giving her a ride.

"*Hola*, Papi," she said.

"This isn't the way you normally walk home from school," I said. "And it's late—it's almost six. Where were you?"

"Nowhere."

"You must have been *somewhere* because nowhere isn't a place," I said jokingly. Isa didn't answer. She just turned up the music she'd been listening to so that I could hear it in the front seat even through her headphones.

This was the Isa I was used to—not the one from yesterday, when she'd been so chummy. I'd gotten used to the grumpy, distant one, but I couldn't help feeling sad that Isa was all shuttered again.

When we got home, my mom had reheated some of the chickpea stew Isa had made the day before, thrown together a salad, and put some bread on the table.

"Wash your hands, everyone," she said.

We all washed up and sat at the table. For some reason Isa refused to meet my eyes. I didn't know if I had done or said something to upset her. Was she mad that we'd picked her up?

That couldn't be it. It was cold out, and it was not a short walk home. Was it because she'd been someplace she didn't want us to know about? That seemed more likely.

Everyone else was eating happily, and I was surprised to find that Isa's stew tasted even better on the second day.

"This is really good, Isa," I told her.

"It is," she said. Then, after a beat, "Thanks."

After everyone had eaten enough, I decided it was time to make my announcement. After two tries at this already, I was pretty sure I knew how I wanted to handle this one. I was going to be calm, confident, and humble.

"Mami, Papi, I have something to tell you. There's going to be a singing contest for teenagers in Hamilton. The auditions are at the end of next week, and I'd like to try out."

I watched my parents exchange a glance and talk to each other with their eyes for a moment before they responded.

"A contest?" asked my dad. He sounded apprehensive, which seemed strange to me. "What kind of contest?"

"What do you mean? It's a regular singing contest. Kids come and try out with a song they choose themselves, and then the judges vote for a group of ten finalists." I didn't know if that was what he was really asking, since it seemed pretty self-explanatory to me. "Then the ten finalists get to sing on TV, and the viewers choose one winner."

"I see," said my mom. "Well, that sounds interesting. And it's open to anyone?"

"Anyone thirteen to eighteen who wants to go to Hamilton and audition," I said. I was really starting to get confused by all the questions. The Sprinkle Sundays sisters and my bandmates had not asked so many. They had just skipped right to the part where they'd been really excited for me. I could feel myself suddenly getting nervous.

"That could be a whole lot of kids," my mother continued. "How many do they think will show up?"

How many do they think will show up? What kind of question was that? Why weren't my parents just saying, "Go, Sierra! You can do it!"?

I took a deep breath and reminded myself to stay calm, confident, and humble. "Um, I have no idea," I said. "A lot, probably."

34

"And you're sure this is something you want to do?" my father asked.

At this point I needed help. I tried to meet Isa's eyes, but she wouldn't look at me. She was the one who'd given me the flyer and told me about it and gotten me all pumped up to do it! Now she needed to step in and say something. But clearly she wasn't going to.

I took another deep breath. My feelings were hurt, but I tried not to show it. I wanted to appear grown-up and professional, since I was asking to try out for something that seemed grown-up and professional.

"Are you guys saying you don't think I'm g-good enough?"

My voice broke a bit on the word "good." So much for grown-up. I sounded like a four-year-old.

It seemed to wake Isa from her mood. "Of *course* you're good enough, Sisi. You're a really good singer. And you're a natural! You've never even had real lessons. You should definitely try out."

And with that, she stared at our parents, as if daring them to contradict her.

"We know you're a wonderful singer!" my mom

said quickly. "I enjoy your singing every day, Sierra. It's one of my favorite sounds."

She looked over at my dad. He said, "It's just that we want to make sure you realize how highly competitive this is likely to be. It could draw contestants from all over. It's one thing to sing with your friends, but it's another to try out in a contest with many contestants, who are all terrific singers like you, and might be taking private voice lessons."

Then my mom said, "We're not telling you *not* to do it! That's your decision. And we're your number one supporters, no matter what. We're just helping you think it through, that's all."

I was quiet for a moment, thinking about my parents' words. By now I understood what they were really concerned about. They didn't want my hopes and dreams to be crushed if I didn't win. They wanted me to be brave but also realistic.

I felt much better.

"I get it," I said, my voice returning to normal. "I know it's going to be competitive and that everyone there will probably be a really terrific singer. But that's okay! I think it'll be a good experience. And I *love* singing. I want to find out if I really have some talent or not. And I think this will help me. I'm going to do it!"

Isa cheered and put her hands up in the air in a *V* for "victory."

My dad's face broke into a huge smile. "Of course you are, my sweet Sierra. And we'll all be there to cheer you on!"

I couldn't believe how relieved I felt. No matter what choice I made, it would never feel right unless I had my family's support. They were the most important people in the world to me.

"You've only got ten days until the audition, so I guess you'll need to get upstairs and practice right after dinner," said Isa. "I'll do the dishes."

I looked at her gratefully. Even though my twin could be distant, she also came through for me when it mattered.

Up in my room I began pulling out my homework, thinking it might be best to get that out of the way before I looked through my songs to see which one would be good for the contest. As I was working on my language arts assignment, I heard Isa come upstairs. Her mood had been all over the place this afternoon—weird and evasive when we'd picked her up, quiet at the table, then supportive to me with my parents, then generous in helping with the dishes.

"Isa?" I called out. "Can you come in here?"

Isa came to my doorway, surveying the absolute tornado that was my room. Even Marshmallow the cat seemed disgusted as she picked her way around the piles on my floor.

"This is bad, even for you," Isa said. She was the only member of the Perez family who preferred to be neat. Her room was always spotless, and she vacuumed it once a week like clockwork.

"Where were you coming from this afternoon?" I asked her, point-blank.

I could see her tense up.

"Nowhere. Why?"

"Isa! Why won't you tell me? I'm not going to get you in trouble or anything. What were you doing? Did you have detention?"

"Oh sure," she said. "Assume it was something bad! Something I'd get in trouble for."

That made me feel awful. I hadn't meant it to sound that way. "I just meant that your secret is safe with me. I'm your twin."

Isa shrugged. "Yeah, well, I don't have any secrets, so don't worry about it. You just focus on you, and everything will be fine."

I was definitely getting the brush-off. But I knew that being vulnerable was the one thing that could get Isa to open up sometimes. So I said, "Isa, I'm nervous."

"Good. It's healthy to be nervous." She turned and left, heading back down the hall. I heard her open the door to her room. A second later she called out, "You're a good singer, Sierra. I'd tell you if you weren't."

"Thanks, sis," I yelled back.

"You're welcome, Sunshine."

CHAPTER FIVE

PEG AND MARY'S ICE CREAM MUSEUM AND FACTORY

Between homework and thinking about which song to sing for the contest next week, you'd think I'd be too busy or nervous to take a field trip for a whole afternoon. But there was nothing that could stand in the way of me, my Sprinkle Sundays sisters, and a tour of the ice cream factory.

Mrs. Shear picked Tamiko and me up from MLK right after dismissal. Allie was already waiting in the back seat, as Vista Green got out twenty minutes before we did.

Tamiko and I climbed into the car, trying to maneuver our overstuffed backpacks so that all three of us could sit together in the back and still have room for our legs. It was a tough squeeze. We wiggled closer together.

I laughed. "This was easier when we were all eight, and a lot smaller!"

Mrs. Shear laughed as well. "You know, someone *could* sit up front with me. I don't have cooties. Or you can all pile your backpacks up here if you'd like."

That's what we did. We threw our bags into the front and buckled our seat belts, and then Mrs. Shear headed in the direction of the highway.

"ROAD TRIP!" yelled Tamiko, rolling her window down.

"We're going on a roooooad trrrrriiiiip," I sang loudly. I hummed a little tune to go with it. "This is a great opportunity for me to warm up for *you know what* next week."

Allie nodded and winked at me. I think she could guess that I didn't want to mention it to Mrs. Shear. I'd decided for the time being to just tell my besties, my band, and my family.

Tamiko drummed her hands on her lap. It was clear how excited we all were not only to be seeing one another on a Tuesday, which rarely happened, but also to be going on an adventure together.

"I thought about this *all day*," said Allie. "In homeroom Colin asked me if I had the notes from our life science class the other day, and I told him I had absolutely no idea. I couldn't even remember because all I could think about was this trip and the wonderful, amazing new flavors we're going to come up with!"

"I've planned ahead," said Tamiko, snapping the fabric on her legs. "I'm wearing realllllly stretchy leggings in case I taste-test too many flavors."

"That was smart," I told her. "I planned ahead too. I did some extra homework last night, so I can just relax and have fun today!"

Mrs. Shear put the radio on, and the three of us sang along to the music. I was good at staying in tune but not always good about remembering the lyrics to certain songs. That was Allie's strength—maybe because she was such a book-loving, word-loving person. She knew the lyrics to everything!

The drive was more than an hour, but with my two besties in the car, and school chatter and gossip to catch up on, the car trip flew by. It felt like no time at all before we were pulling up to a giant, hand-painted sign that read, PEG AND MARY'S ICE CREAM

MUSEUM AND FACTORY. We all let out a squeal.

There was a visitor's lot, and Mrs. Shear pulled in there.

"Are we ready, girls?" she asked.

"READY!" we replied as one.

"I think I was born for this moment," said Tamiko. "I can't wait to be inspired! I bet I can come up with three awesome new flavors after this visit. Maybe four."

Mrs. Shear patted her arm. "You always come up with brilliant ideas, Tamiko. Not to worry. We've just been in a dry spell."

We followed the signs to the welcome center. There was a thirty-minute guided tour of the factory, and a store where you could taste-test and also buy ice cream. We decided to take the tour first.

The tour was even more interesting than I'd thought it would be. Because Peg and Mary's was a national brand, they had a huge factory. The main room of the factory was enormous—with endless conveyor belts, huge commercial mixing vats, more vats filled with ingredients, and signs everywhere about wearing protective clothing and keeping your hair covered and how to improve employee safety. We could see employees in white coats walking around checking on things as the mixtures went down each conveyor belt to the final vat at the end, where it was mixed and then separated and put into containers. It was nothing like the small-batch production that Mrs. Shear did. It was overwhelming, really.

"This is fascinating," Mrs. Shear said. "And it certainly makes you think about where your food comes from, doesn't it?"

"Yes!" said Allie. "Who knew this many people and machines went into making one small pint of ice cream?"

As we strolled around the perimeter of the room, I started humming one of the songs we'd heard on the radio on the way there. It was the kind of pop song that got stuck in your head and wouldn't leave. I only knew the words to the chorus, but I thought maybe it would make a good audition piece for the contest.

"What are you humming, Sierra?" asked Tamiko. "Is it 'Too Good for You'? I love that song!"

I nodded. "Yes. I was just thinking about singing it next week for"—I lowered my voice so Mrs. Shear wouldn't hear me—"the *thing*. You know."

Tamiko gave me a funny look, as if wondering why

I didn't just say "the singing contest." Allie seemed to have understood earlier. And now that we were in the factory, I especially didn't want Mrs. Shear to think I wasn't focusing on the tour and the flavors and coming up with some new ideas. This was a work trip, and I wanted her to know I took it seriously.

Tamiko nodded at me vaguely and turned her attention back to the tour guide, who was explaining that the United States was one of the top three countries in the world in terms of ice cream consumption. No surprise there! She also told us that chocolate was the first flavor ever invented, not vanilla, as most people assumed, and that the average number of licks it takes to get through a one-scoop cone of ice cream is fifty.

"I'm learning so much!" Allie exclaimed. "I always felt like an ice cream expert, but I feel like an ice cream mega-expert now."

Next we were led into a room filled with ice cream toppings. It was absolutely beautiful. I didn't know where to look—there was so much to see! Many things I'd never even thought of as ice cream toppings before, like ground coffee, bacon, and saltine crackers.

"You guys have SO many toppings and

ingredients!" Allie said to the tour guide. "How do you keep track of your inventory to keep it fresh? I mean, do you ever buy too much, or too little? What happens when you make a mistake in your ordering?"

As soon as she'd finished speaking, Allie's eyes went wide. She added quickly, "Am I asking too many questions?"

The tour guide laughed. "I love all your questions, *and* your enthusiasm. And yes, of course, inventory and ordering are an imperfect science, even at a factory as large and busy as this one. So we don't think of the inevitable inventory fluctuations as mistakes—we look at them as a challenge to come up with brand-new flavors!"

"I love that!" I said. "I'm all about having a positive outlook."

Some of the others in our tour group were milling around the room now, but Tamiko, Allie, Mrs. Shear, and I were sticking close to the guide. I guess she could tell that we were truly interested in all the inventory talk, because she went on.

"Have you ladies ever heard of the book *Beautiful Oops!*?" she asked.

We all shook our heads.

"It shares a theory—an understanding, really— that anything that goes wrong while you're creating art can be turned into something *beautiful*. Now, let's say someone wants cherry vanilla ice cream but we've run out of cherries. We'll see what we do have and recommend something else, presenting it as, 'We're out of cherries, but how about trying our newest delicious flavor, vanilla banana peanut butter chip? It's sure to knock your socks off!'"

Allie laughed. "That's because you probably have lots of bananas and peanut butter chips, right?"

The guide nodded. "Exactly."

"Tamiko does that naturally!" I said, squeezing Tamiko's arm. "She's been beautiful-oops-ing without even knowing it."

Mrs. Shear smiled. "She has. And come to think of it, I've definitely had to beautiful-oops it myself a few times when I'm making some of our old standbys and I've run out of an ingredient."

The tour guide nodded. "I think it's a great thing to remember for life in general, not just for recipes. If something goes wrong, beautiful-oops it!"

I loved the idea of the beautiful oops. I was always getting into one tricky situation or another, juggling social commitments, sports, and academic groups. When I got in over my head, I just needed to find a way to make it work and carry on.

I started humming to myself again, thinking in the back of my mind what a neat concept beautiful oops could be for a Wildflowers song. I'd have to talk to Tessa about the lyrics, because she was so good at them.

I kept humming as we followed the guide to the next room. Tamiko and Allie were walking ahead of me, and I saw Tamiko lean her head toward Allie and whisper something. Allie quickly nodded and whispered something back. Then they turned around at the same time and looked at me.

I immediately stopped humming. "What's up?" I asked.

Allie shrugged and looked pointedly at Tamiko again, who smiled. Neither answered me. They just kept walking.

I followed, utterly confused. That was so weird! We were not the type of three-person friendship that kept secrets or talked about one another. That was part of the Sprinkle Sundays sisters code. And just now Allie and Tamiko had been *very* obviously talking about me.

I decided to push it out of my mind for now, because I was probably just paranoid or giddy from the nearness of so much ice cream. I focused on the Flavoroom instead, which included all the different flavors that Peg and Mary had ever made, including ones that they didn't sell anymore. They even had a clipboard where visitors could sign their name if they wanted a certain "dead" flavor brought back to life.

I moseyed up and down the rows, enjoying reading all the different flavors. I knew something would come to me if I just thought about it long enough, and I wanted to be able to give Mrs. Shear at least one really good new flavor idea before we left the factory.

Peppery Peach? Moroccan Mango? Peanut Butter and Jelly-icious? Nothing seemed quite right.

The song from the car ride, "Too Good for You," popped back into my head, and I sang it very softly under my breath as I wound my way around the room. I liked the tour, but I was pretty sure that after thirty minutes of nothing but *talking* about ice cream, I was ready to move on to tasting some of it. Visiting the ice cream store for tasting flavors and buying cones and pints was next. I was ready.

Still humming as I signed my name to the list for

the long-gone flavor Chunky Chunky Coconut, I happened to look up and see Allie and Tamiko whispering and eyeing me again. The second they noticed that I saw them, they stopped and started talking loudly about the Gotta Have Goat Cheese flavor.

"Chicas!" I said. *"What* is going on?"

Allie's face turned completely beet red, but Tamiko pasted on a big smile and said, "Nothing, Sierra! Just looking for inspiration."

There was a moment of total silence after she spoke. I knew she wasn't being truthful, and she and Allie knew that I knew it.

It was something about me. Had I been acting weird? I'd mentioned the contest a few times. But I hadn't made a big deal about it, had I? Was I boring everyone to death with it after just two days?

I supposed I *had* made a huge deal about it the day before when I'd made Tamiko video-chat with Allie during lunch so I could tell everyone at the same time. I'd acted like I had big news—like I'd already won the contest—when really all I'd done was find out about it and decide to enter. All I'd really done was read a flyer.

I didn't want to be a drama queen. Especially after

Tamiko's recent queen-of-everything phase. I just wanted to be my nice, sunny Sierra self. The one my friends didn't whisper about.

At last the tour guide announced that it was time to move on to the tasting.

But it no longer sounded enticing to me. My stomach felt queasy. Suddenly the field trip didn't seem quite as fun anymore.

I wanted to go home.

CHAPTER SIX
THE RIGHT SONG

None of us came up with the perfect new flavor for Molly's after our tour, but Mrs. Shear was really happy with how much we had all learned from it. She reminded us that sometimes ideas take a few days to "ferment." Then Tamiko suggested Fermented Froot Loops as a flavor, and everyone laughed.

Tamiko and Allie acted completely normal on the way home from the factory, so I tried to act normal too. But inside I was worried. I could tell when something was going on and I was being left out. Most people can sense things like that. And when you're dealing with two girls you've been best friends with for years and years, it's even easier to tell.

I didn't want to outright ask them what was up

again in front of Mrs. Shear in the car, because I thought that would make everyone uncomfortable, so I decided to just put it out of my mind until I saw them together again at Molly's on Sunday. If things weren't back to normal by then, I'd deal with it.

For the time being I had to focus on myself and preparing for the contest next week. Luckily, Reagan had confirmed with everyone in the band that we'd be having an extra rehearsal after school on Wednesday. I was really touched that everyone could spare an extra day to help me prepare. I knew they all had schedules as busy as mine, and homework as well.

I arrived ten minutes early for our practice, which was practically unheard of for me. But that's how much I cared about the contest. I'd even brought the snacks for the day, since Reagan's mom was usually the one to provide them, and I wanted to make sure that we could keep using her garage as our rehearsal space for a long, long time.

I'd stopped at a market on my way there and bought a bunch of muffins and some clementines. My mom always told Isa and me that vitamin C is good for the brain and the body, so I figured it might be good for brainstorming.

Reagan was already on the couch when I arrived, her math textbook open on her lap. "Hello!" she said. "Come in. I was just trying to get a head start on my homework."

I held up the bag of food. "I've got food!"

"Hurray!" she said. "I need it."

Tessa arrived a moment later, wearing her guitar case on her back, followed by Kasey.

"This is an exciting day!" Tessa squealed. "We're going to pick your audition song, which will help you win the contest, which will mean you get to appear on TV, and then you'll mention the Wildflowers, and then we'll get tons of requests for gigs, and we'll be so busy being rock stars that we'll have to drop out of eighth grade!"

We all laughed, Tessa included.

Kasey collapsed onto the couch, looking like she'd had a pretty long day. I handed her the pack of muffins and clementines, and she took one of each. "So, where do we begin?" she asked.

I threw my hands up. "I have no idea! I really need you all. I've had different songs running through my head for days, and I don't know how to decide which one would be the best for me to perform."

Reagan peeled a clementine, looking thoughtful. "Well, *I* think we need to strategize."

Kasey nodded. "I agree. This isn't just about picking a song you like. That's easy! This is a *contest*. This is about making an *impression*. What type of song will make the best impression? A trendy pop hit? Something more rock? An original, or a cover?"

Tessa shook her head. "I don't think it's about the specific song as much as finding the song that best suits Sierra's *voice* so that her voice is what they hear."

Reagan nodded. "I agree. Totally. It's about her voice."

I was just about to agree with Reagan, when she spoke again.

"Actually, now that I think about it, maybe it's *not* just about her voice. Maybe they're looking for someone marketable, too. So we need to present you as a *package*. You know, with a very distinct sense of style in your clothes, your voice, your song choice. Someone that they know could become famous at some point, so they can say they discovered you."

"That's true too," said Kasey. "But what's MOST important is that you leave them wanting more. You want them to say, 'Hey, that Sierra was really talented. I want to hear more from her.'"

"Okay, stop!" I said. "Now I'm totally freaking out! How can I possibly put together a style, pick a song that exemplifies my style, practice the song and sing it perfectly, and also exude star quality, all in just a week? I can't do it!"

I wedged myself into the couch beside Kasey and put my head in my hands.

Reagan put her arm around me. "Maybe we're taking things a little too far," she said. She rubbed her hand up and down my arm soothingly, like a mom. "How about for today we just have you sing a few of the songs that we all think you sing best, and we'll vote? And *your* vote counts the most, obviously." She grinned at me.

"That's right!" agreed Kasey. "All that other stuff doesn't matter if you don't love the song you're singing. The judges will feel that. What's your favorite song?"

"And try to make it a happy one," Tessa chimed in. "I do think judges give extra points to people who seem happy."

I racked my brain. Happy, favorite song. Happy. Favorite. Song.

I shook my head and buried it in my hands again. "I can't think of a single song!"

Reagan passed me her binder of original Wildflowers songs and covers that we've done, and I began flipping through it. There were so many great songs in there. How could I pick just one?

"You look like you're agonizing," Reagan said. "How about you do what Tessa suggested—sing something that makes people happy. Something sunny, like you. Then you can't go wrong."

If she'd said that to me first thing, and everyone had agreed and left it at that, then maybe I could have done that. But after hearing so many suggestions and ideas about what to prioritize in picking a song, and all of it sounding so *right*, I was truly and completely baffled.

I *had* to have the right song. That much was clear.

"If you have fun, they'll have fun," said Kasey. "For now let's just sing a few random songs and see if we can't loosen you up. Any practice will be good for your voice, regardless."

"Okay," I said. "That's doable. Let's start with 'Stand Up, Speak Up' because that song always makes me feel good."

57

For the next hour or so, we ran through a bunch of different songs. But while everyone agreed that most of them sounded fine, no one thought there was one that stood out in particular. Not even me.

So we wrapped up our emergency practice with our emergency unresolved. I thought about calling Allie and Tamiko and asking their opinion about what I should sing, but when I picked up my phone, I immediately put it back down again. They didn't know our song list as well as my Wildflowers bandmates, and there was still that yucky feeling in my stomach from them talking about me the day before.

It looked like I'd have to figure this out on my own.

My mom picked me up from practice and told me that dinner wouldn't be ready for at least an hour, so I went straight to my room to pore over my song choices again. I was hearing so many songs in my head at this point—from rehearsal and from the radio—that I was starting to go a little nuts.

I plopped onto my bed and started scrolling through my phone, looking at song titles. Then I heard something odd. It sounded like *me*, singing a

Wildflowers song from somewhere in the house. It was very brief—just ten seconds or so—but I heard it. Weird. Was Isa listening to a tape of me singing?

I opened my door and went out into the hallway. Isa's door was shut. I knocked on it.

"Who is it?" she called.

"The queen of England," I responded. "Seriously, Isa. Do you really have to ask?"

"Yes, I do," she said. I could hear the exasperation in her voice. "Come in."

I went in and found her sitting on her bed, her phone in her hand, just as I'd been sitting moments before. It was a common thing to do, of course, but I was still sometimes struck by our twin-ness showing itself in various ways when I wasn't expecting it.

"Did you come in here to stare at me, or can I help you with something?" Isa asked.

I rolled my eyes. "Knock it off, Isa. I came in because I heard myself singing! Were you playing a track of me doing a Wildflowers song?"

She shook her head hard. "*No.* The whole world doesn't revolve around *you*, Sierra. I was watching something on YouTube, though. Maybe it just sounded familiar."

59

She sounded overly defensive. Was what I'd asked so wrong? Or was Isa right—was I acting like the world revolved around me? I didn't *think* I was, but it was possible. And that theory made sense, considering what had happened with Allie and Tamiko the day before.

"I guess I was wrong," I said. "It's funny, though—it sounded just like me."

I turned to leave. Then Isa called, "Wait."

I looked back at her expectantly.

"Did you pick your song yet for the contest?" she asked.

Now it was my turn to sound exasperated. "I wish. I have *no idea* what to sing. I just met with the Wildflowers and we spent more than an hour going through songs, and no one could agree on what type of song I should sing, or if I should do a cover or an original, or focus on what suits my voice best, or which one makes me more of a 'package' . . ."

I let my voice trail off. I was pretty sure Isa was going to just nod and dismiss me, but instead she said, "You didn't ask me."

I stared at her. "You don't even like the kind of music I sing."

"Maybe I don't. But I *am* the one who told you about the competition. Don't you think I want you to do well? I'm your sister!"

Tamiko and Allie had seemed very happy for me the other day, but now something was up. So they were no help. My bandmates were wonderful and well-meaning and dying to help me, but they were too full of excitement to be very useful at the moment. Maybe I needed someone blunt and opinionated and practical like Isa to steer me.

"You're right. I *do* need you, Isa. I'm worried I'm going to try to be so many different things for the judges that I'll just end up a big, hot mess onstage and embarrass myself."

"We can't have that," she said, sliding her phone into the top drawer of her nightstand. "You represent Team Perez, and I'm not going to let Team Perez be embarrassed on TV."

"Only the finalists make it onto TV," I reminded her. I fussed with my hair nervously.

"Whatever. There will be tons of people at the audition, listening and watching. This is big, Sisi. Let's get to work."

CHAPTER SEVEN

WHAT'S THE SPECIAL?

Somehow the old Isa had returned. I didn't know if it was because she was proud that she'd found the contest and given me the idea to try out, or because she liked that I was asking her opinion about things again, or if she was just in a really good mood because her travel soccer team was doing well.

But every night that week after we were both home from our activities and had finished our homework and dinner, she came into my room and curled up on my bed with our two cats and watched me practice different songs. She listened intently, like she really cared, and offered interesting, honest feedback about each one. She was still Isa enough to tell me the truth and not fluff me up with compliments.

However, no matter how many times I asked her to, she refused to pick out my song for me. Desperate, I even went downstairs and sang for our parents a few of the songs I was considering, but they wouldn't pick for me either.

Everyone kept telling me that this was *my* audition, and it needed to be *my* decision. But I was getting more and more tired of trying to make this decision. I had my ever-increasing pile of schoolwork to do, my soccer and softball practices, I was doing the lighting again for the school play, and I wanted someone to just *tell* me what to do!

There was some good news, though. At school all week Tamiko was acting completely normally. She and MacKenzie and I ate and talked together every day at lunch, and I saw Tamiko between classes and in science, the one subject we had together. And it was like nothing weird had ever happened at the ice cream factory. Allie had been texting me normally too, sending me pictures of her incredibly delicious Vista Green lunches, like fish tacos and microgreens, instead of the same old sloppy joes we had at MLK.

So at least that was off my mind for the moment.

Well, maybe not off my mind, but it seemed like things were okay.

But when Sunday finally rolled around and it was time for my regular weekly shift at Molly's again, I was reluctant to go. I felt better about my friends, but the contest was just four days away, and I still hadn't chosen a song. As I was heading out the door to walk to work, Reagan texted me, Did you pick the song yet? Do you want to have another emergency practice?

I wrote back, No song yet. Please—just tell me what to do!

She replied, Whatever you pick will be great. You are great! But you need to pick ASAP. OKAY???

I sighed as I read her text and walked slowly across town. As I was crossing Main Street to turn off to the street for Molly's, I felt a funny little skip in my stomach. I turned around, wondering what it was that might be bothering me. And for just a second I saw a girl in all black with a baseball cap on her head walking into the Middle C music shop across the square. I felt the funny skip again when I saw her.

Could it have been Isa?

There were other girls who wore all black. And

Isa and I were both average height. Not many people had Isa's hair, though, which was a mostly grown-out fauxhawk with purple tips. But this girl had her hair up in a cap, something Isa never ever did. She liked hoodies, but she did not like hats.

Still, my old twin-tuition, which was what Isa and I called the special spidey-sense we had for each other, was telling me that it was her. What was she doing in the music store? Looking at instruments?

I shook my head and picked up the pace so that I wouldn't be late for work. Being late was something I was famous for, and it wasn't exactly like being famous for singing!

"I'm here!" I called as I breezed into Molly's. The bell over the door tinkled in greeting, and I saw that the clock read 12:45. Whew. Made to work exactly on time without a minute to spare.

Tamiko was serving a customer an ice cream cone as Allie wrote a new recommendation up on the daily pairings board.

"Try reading Roald Dahl's *James and the Giant Peach* with our Beaches and Cream flavor! Mmmm, beachy!"

"Great idea!" I told Allie, giving her a thumbs-up.

"Isa and I loved all the Roald Dahl books when we were little."

"Me too," said Allie. She glanced out the window at the beautiful sunny afternoon and said, "And doesn't today seem like a peachy day?"

I nodded enthusiastically, even though I didn't feel all that peachy inside. I was too worried about the approaching contest.

"Hey, has either one of you ever been in the Middle C music store across the square?" I asked.

Tamiko nodded. "Yes, I have. I used to take piano, remember? My parents bought all my sheet music there."

"I probably have too, just not for a long time. Why?" Allie asked.

I thought about mentioning seeing Isa, then decided against it. It seemed a little odd to say, "I thought I saw my twin sister, but I didn't go over to check and see if it was her. Do you guys think it was her?"

I should have just walked over there right then, but I would have ended up being late to work.

"No reason," I said. "I was just, um, wondering if they had a good selection of song music in there."

I busied myself straightening the napkins and plastic spoons. No matter how many times a day we tidied those, they were always askew.

"I guess that means you're still looking for a song to sing for the contest?" Tamiko said. "Maybe Allie and I can help. Sing a few of your favorites for us. Molly's is the perfect venue for an impromptu concert."

Allie nodded. "Sing something! There aren't any customers in here now. We might as well help you."

My face broke into a huge grin. My friends *did* want to help me! "Thanks, guys, but since we're at work, I probably should be focusing on work. Anyway, I've given it a lot of thought, and even though I WANT someone else to pick my song for me, I think it's best that I decide on my own."

Tamiko nodded. "I think you're right. That way, no matter what happens, you won't blame anyone else. . . ."

No matter what happens? Was Tamiko saying I'd lose and then blame someone else for picking my song? And did she not really believe I had a chance to win?

That hurt. I stayed silent, which was very unlike me. Allie noticed immediately and jumped in. "She

67

didn't mean it like *that*, Sierra. Just that this is your audition, so you should make all the choices for it. Because you're representing *you*, you know?"

I nodded, still not trusting my voice. Tamiko's cheeks flushed, but she said, "Sierra knows I didn't mean it like that."

Just then Mrs. Shear came out into the front of the shop. She had a knack for appearing whenever there was a tense moment. I was pretty sure it wasn't a coincidence.

"Hello, lovely girls! Are you all just bursting with ideas for new flavors for Molly's?"

The three of us looked at one another sheepishly. None of us had even discussed it since our trip on Tuesday. I knew that I personally hadn't given the new ice cream flavor a single thought all week. I'd been much too preoccupied. I felt terrible.

Mrs. Shear pointed at the specials board. "Tamiko, what's going on? The specials board is still bare!"

Tamiko, who was never at a loss for words, opened her mouth, but nothing came out. Even if she had just hurt my feelings by accident, I felt the need to defend her.

"Um, well," I started to say. "Remember how

there was that neat room with the toppings? Maybe we could have a special just called Toppings, and it would just be . . . a cone full of toppings?"

Ugh. Even I thought that sounded weak.

Mrs. Shear smiled politely but shook her head. "That's creative, but it doesn't really help us sell our homemade ice cream, which is the goal. Other ideas? We need a real winner here, people!"

Then something odd happened. Allie looked over at Tamiko, and the two of them grinned at each other. Hugely. It was a weird, private grin, just like the one at the factory. I think Tamiko might have even winked at Allie.

Were they smiling about my dumb idea? *What was happening?* Whatever it was, there was some private secret that I was left out of. That much was for sure.

It felt like the ice cream factory tour all over again. And I wasn't imagining it—I could see it with my own eyes.

Uncomfortable, I looked down at the case full of bins of ice cream. I counted them over and over again, trying to calm my nerves. A minute or two passed and no one spoke.

"This isn't like you guys!" said Mrs. Shear,

shaking her head. "Tamiko, you always have something up your sleeve."

Tamiko rubbed her chin and looked thoughtful. "We could do design-your-own sundaes again. They were a big hit."

Allie nodded vigorously. "They were. We sold a ton!"

Mrs. Shear sighed. "I guess. I was just hoping for some of that Sprinkle Sundays sisters magic . . . like with those mermaid sundaes, and Coffee and Doughnuts, and some of your other ideas."

"We'll keep working on it," I promised. I felt terrible about not having thought of the new flavor at all this week. Especially since Mrs. Shear had been so nice to take us on that field trip! "I promise. We'll come up with something amazing!"

Tamiko nudged Allie, and they looked at each other knowingly again. I wanted to shout, "WHY ARE YOU DOING THAT?" but I kept my mouth tightly shut until Mrs. Shear left on a run to the store for more walnuts and shaved almonds.

"Guys, what is going *on*?" I finally said. I did not like confrontation, especially with my two besties, but this was ridiculous. "You look like you have a secret, and I'm not in on it. If I'm being annoying about the contest or something, please—just tell me. I can take it. You guys are making me nervous."

"Oh, Sierra, no!" Allie said, sounding worried. "That's not it at all. We're totally pumped for you to try out for the singing contest. We just . . . Well, we have an idea about something, and we're still working on it, and we'll tell you when it's ready."

She looked nervously at Tamiko, who nodded confidently. "Yes, we'll tell you soon. Don't worry—it's nothing bad."

My dad once told me that when someone says, "Don't worry—it's nothing bad," it is *always* something bad, so he never ever says that to his pet patients' owners. He always says, "Here's what's going on," and just tells them the truth straight-out.

It seemed that there were a lot of secrets going on. Where Isa had been last week when Papi and I had picked her up, why she'd been going to Middle C instead of her soccer practice earlier, and why Allie and Tamiko were cooking something up without me when normally I was involved in all of their schemes.

I loved being busy and social and spending time with all my different groups of friends. And because I was so busy all the time, I did occasionally miss some things with my besties—like trips to the movies or study dates or whatever. But missing something and being left out of something were two very different experiences.

"Fine," I said at last, because Allie and Tamiko were watching me carefully, waiting for me to say something. And what else could I say? They weren't being mean. They just weren't being their usual selves. "Let's just get to work, I guess."

Allie started wiping counters, and Tamiko added, "Back by popular demand—design your own sundae!" to our specials board, even though we all knew it wasn't as good as coming up with something new and unique. And I got my phone out and put on a playlist of music that would be fun and cheerful for customers when they came in. It soon got busy, and I relaxed slightly. I was in my element, greeting customers and adding up their orders in my head without using the register. However, in the back of my mind, I couldn't help wondering what on Earth I was going to sing on Thursday for the audition, and why my two best friends were keeping something from me.

CHAPTER EIGHT
ISA'S SECRET

I walked home slowly from work, keeping an eye out for Isa. I seemed to see her everywhere lately, instead of nowhere, which was how it had been for months and months.

Allie and Tamiko had been mostly normal for the rest of our shift at Molly's, so I'd focused on being sunshiny Sierra—even though I hadn't felt like it—and making sure our customers were happy.

But I'd also made a decision. Tonight I would pick my song, no matter what, because I needed to spend the next few days singing it nonstop if I was going to be ready for the audition. Even if I had to put a bunch of song names into a hat and pick one out randomly, I was going to make a decision! Tonight!

When I got home, I could smell good things cooking in the kitchen. Sundays really were the best.

"Hola!" I called out.

Papi answered. "*Hola*, Sierra. I'm making masitas and rice. Dinner will be ready in an hour or so."

"Yum! *Gracias*, Papi." I thudded up the stairs and went straight to my room.

One hour was perfect. That gave me just enough time to look through my songs one more time and try to pick one. Then I could begin practicing it after dinner. And stick with it.

I flopped onto my bed with the Wildflowers songbook and began paging through it. The fact that my bandmates had all personally chosen each of these songs made the decision even harder. We loved all the songs to begin with, and on top of that I had special memories of us playing them together. They were *all* my favorite song!

I hummed a song, a pop hit from the radio, just something to warm up my vocal cords as I looked. When I heard a sound from the hallway, my head popped up, and there was Isa walking by with her laundry basket, only she wasn't wearing all black. She was in a black T-shirt, but she had blue jeans on with it. For her, that was unusual.

"Hey—were you wearing that all day?" I asked.

Isa paused in my doorway, holding the basket in front of her. "Huh?"

"Were you wearing black leggings earlier?"

"I don't know." She narrowed her eyes. "Maybe. Why?"

It was the new Isa, the infuriating one. "Never mind. I thought I saw you walking into Middle C at the main square earlier."

And then I saw it—Isa's entire face bloomed a bright red and she practically ran down the hallway.

"Isa!" I called. "STOP. Get back here!"

I ran into the hall and grabbed at her shirtsleeve before she could escape to the basement laundry room. "Come in here," I said, pulling her into my room and shutting the door.

Surprisingly, she let me.

"What's going on?" I asked. "And don't tell me 'nothing.' Why were you at Middle C? And why have you been acting so ... *Old Isa* lately? And where were you the other day when Papi and I picked you up?"

I fully expected her to say, "None of your business,

Sunshine," and run off again, but she didn't. Instead she put her laundry basket on the floor and sat down on my bed.

"Okay," she said. "I'll tell you. But you can't tell anyone—not even Mami and Papi. Promise?"

I felt my stomach drop. What was going on? Was Isa in serious trouble?

"I can't promise that," I said. "What if it's something serious or you're in danger? I'd have to tell them."

Isa burst out laughing. "In *danger*? Me? What do you think I've been *doing*?"

I threw my hands up, frustrated. "I have no idea! That's the problem!"

"Well, calm yourself." Isa lowered her voice and said, "I've been taking . . . singing lessons."

My jaw dropped to my knees. At first I was sure she was teasing, but her face was deadly serious.

"*Singing lessons?* That's the big secret?"

She nodded, looking solemn. "I found a teacher at Middle C, and he's giving me a discounted rate since I told him I'm paying for the lessons myself. I've been going for a few weeks."

"But . . . why wouldn't you tell us that? I think it's great that you're singing!"

Isa rolled her eyes. "Do you think I want everyone comparing us? You're in a band—everyone knows you're a great singer. I don't want to be the twin with the worse voice."

I thought about that. Isa and I both played soccer, but she played on a travel boys' team, while I played on MLK's eighth-grade girls' team. I knew that she was much better than I was, and while I was proud of her, I guess sometimes it did feel weird. Being identical twins makes a lot of things awkward.

"Yeah, I get that," I said. "I *love* that you're interested in singing, though. I'd be happy to practice with you. . . ."

Isa shook her head. "NO! I mean, not yet. Let me practice a little and get better. I'm still learning."

"Okay," I said. "That's fair." Then something occurred to me. "Hey, was that a recording of *you* I heard you playing in your room the other day? The one that I thought was me?"

Isa grinned shyly. "Yeah. I was singing one of your Wildflowers songs—just for myself, to see how it sounded."

"Isa! I can't believe you didn't tell me any of this. I think it's awesome. And," I said, pausing, not wanting to push too much, because Isa really didn't like to talk about personal stuff, "it seems to be making you *happier*. You've seemed much happier lately. Singing makes me happy too. I can express how I'm feeling using someone else's words."

Isa nodded. "It does feel good. I wasn't sure if I'd like it—I just wanted to try it—but now that I think I *do* like it, I want to ask Mami and Papi to help me pay for more lessons."

"I'm sure they will if you just tell them," I said.

"I'm not ready yet," she said forcefully. "So *don't* say anything. Got it?"

"Got it."

"Let's talk about you," Isa said. "You obviously don't have a song yet, right?"

I shook my head.

"Or an outfit?"

I shook my head again.

"Let's work on that. Start pulling stuff out of your closet and trying it on. I'll look at your songs."

It was a relief to not have to make these decisions myself. Even though Isa and I didn't share each other's tastes, she would never let me embarrass myself in public.

I laid a bunch of outfit options out on the floor to show her. "This yellow blouse is bright, so it will look good on camera," I said. "And this purple striped dress is good, because it's a dress, so it looks like I dressed up and I'm taking the audition seriously. And then I have this fun T-shirt that the Wildflowers and I made for one our shows—"

"Which outfit do *you* like best?" she asked.

I had no idea. I liked them all, and I said so. "I do get a lot of compliments when I wear the purple dress, though."

"Don't worry too much about what other people think. Which outfit would make *you* feel good, and make you feel the most like yourself? Because that confidence will help you perform better. If you're just wearing something other people like, you won't be one-hundred-percent comfortable, and it will show. I know, because everyone wants me to dress like you, in bright colors, but I know that I'm happier in black. Also, I look awesome in it."

She grinned, and I grinned back. I felt a huge swell of gratitude for my twin sister.

"C'mon, Sierra. Which outfit makes YOU feel good?" Isa said again. "Makes you feel the most like yourself?"

The answer to that was easy—it was the Wildflowers T-shirt I'd made with my band. I'd hand-painted it with wildflowers, and it had all my favorite colors on it. Plus, it was one-of-a-kind.

I pointed to the T-shirt. "This shirt makes me feel so happy, because it reminds me of my band and how much fun we have together! And I could wear it with a denim skirt and bright tights, to really make it a 'Sierra' outfit. What do you think?"

It was almost inconceivable—me asking Isa for fashion advice. But I knew she'd give me an honest answer.

"Sounds perfect, Sisi. That's exactly what you want—to be yourself and feel like yourself up there. That's what the judges want too. They want to meet the authentic you."

Suddenly a light bulb went off in my mind. I knew exactly which song would go with my outfit, and with me.

I grabbed the songbook off my bed and flipped through it until I found the page. I held it up and showed it to Isa.

"'Be Yourself'?" she read. "Ha! That sounds perfect! That is the exact right song to audition with.

Now all we have to do is have you practice it a few hundred times before Thursday."

"A few hundred?" I squealed. "Isa! I have to go to school."

"I'm not going to let you embarrass Team Perez. Let's get started. Stand up. Smile. Shoulders back. And . . . begin. . . ."

CHAPTER NINE
BE YOURSELF

Finally the day of the audition arrived. My mom picked me, Isa, and Tamiko up from school. Allie was already with her in the car. I was thrilled to have my best friends and my sister there to cheer me on. My dad had wanted to come also, but he'd had to stay at the veterinary clinic.

"I love your outfit," Allie said as I slid in next to her. "It's very Sierra."

I beamed. "That's exactly what I was going for! Isa helped me pick it out."

The three of us Sprinkle Sundays sisters squished into the middle seat of my mother's car, while Isa took the front seat. I was so glad that she wanted to come along. I was even more glad when Tamiko said, "I really like your earrings, Isa. Ear cuffs are huge in Japan right now. I saw a lot of people wearing them when I was there last summer."

Isa nodded and said thank you. I could tell she felt a little awkward around Allie and Tamiko, even though when we were younger, we all played together all the time. But she was trying, and they were trying, and I appreciated it.

The drive to Hamilton was only about twenty minutes, and when we pulled into the parking lot of the community center, it was already packed. A bunch of kids must have left school early in order to show up and get in line. I'd had a geometry test in the afternoon that would have been a pain to miss, but now I wished I'd tried to reschedule it. The butterflies in my stomach were flapping wildly as I looked at how many people were there.

"Stay cool," Isa said, even though I hadn't said a word. "It's just singing. You do it all the time."

"I'm cool," I said. Then I looked at my friends and sister. "No, I'm not! I'm terrified!"

Allie side-hugged me. "You're going to be great. Just . . . be yourself!"

Everyone laughed, and I was so glad that I'd finally settled on that song. It really did seem perfect for the occasion. I wished I'd decided on it sooner so I could have practiced it more, but I'd been singing it in my head all day at school, and at home in the evenings for my parents and Isa. I was as ready as I could be.

After we parked and walked up to the entrance, my mom went to scout out some information about where we should sign in and where we'd be waiting to audition, while Allie, Tamiko, Isa, and I stood in line.

"There are *so many people*," Allie said. "Can you believe it? I had no idea this would be so big."

I shot her a nervous look. "Don't say that! You're making it worse!"

Tamiko shook her head and said dismissively, "Half of these people have probably never sung anything in their lives. They've just watched those singing competitions on TV and decided they could do it too."

"Yeah," agreed Allie. "You're a *real* singer, Sierra. You're in a band!"

Their words were comforting, but I knew that plenty of these kids probably sang a lot as well, in a choir or lessons or wherever.

"You're a good singer, Sisi," said Isa quietly. "You really are."

I squeezed her hand quickly to say *Thank you*. Some of the kids in front of us were goofing around with their friends, talking about school and movies they'd seen and plans for the weekend. But some were holding sheet music and doing vocal warm-ups.

"Do you hear that girl?" I whispered to my crew, pointing with my head at a tall black-haired girl ahead of us in line. "She sounds like an angel. Did you hear that high C?"

Tamiko shrugged. "Angels belong in heaven. We want good singers here on Earth, like *you*, Sierra."

Allie nodded her agreement. "Yeah," she said. "So she hits a really high note. Big deal! Although I do like that boy up there with the raspy voice. He sounds different from everyone else."

"This is a great opportunity for you to sing alongside other good singers," Isa said. "It's just like soccer. Do you want to play against a team that's never won a game? Or play against a strong team so that you can get better?"

"Get better," I said, forcing a brave smile, but inside I was dissolving into nervous little pieces. Had I made a huge mistake deciding to come to this audition?

A person in a blue vest and a name tag that said VOLUNTEER finally made it down the line and handed me a number—eighty-four. I was number eighty-four to try out. And there were still tons of kids behind me. Who knew there were this many local teen singers?

Eventually the line started moving and we were ushered into a large recreation room that had been set up with rows of folding chairs. We could sit anywhere we wanted while we waited. The volunteers came in every so often to call kids in by groups of ten. So I had a while to wait.

I hummed to myself and did some quiet vocal warm-ups. I felt too shy to really belt it out in front of everyone in the room, especially since some of them were so good. So I chatted with Allie, Tamiko, Isa, and my mom, and tried to act as if I had everything under control.

"Want to practice your song?" Allie asked after we'd been waiting for more than an hour. "Or at least whisper-sing it?"

I shook my head. "Not in front of everyone. It'll just make me more nervous."

"You should practice it a few times," Isa said. "Go into the hall or the bathroom."

I looked at her in horror. "But then I might miss my number when they call it! I'd lose my chance."

"I could go in your place," Isa said, deadpan. "Then, when I won, you could go on TV and accept the award."

Allie and Tamiko laughed, certain she was joking, but I just looked at my twin. I wondered if she really *did* want to try out. . . . After all, she'd been taking the voice lessons, and she was the one who'd originally found the flyer for the contest.

I didn't answer for so long that Isa smiled and nudged me with her elbow. "I'm *kidding*. You know I couldn't do this."

"Numbers eighty to eighty-nine, please. Eighty to eighty-nine," someone announced over the microphone.

"That's you!" shrieked Tamiko. "Knock 'em dead, Sierra!"

"Break a leg!" said Allie.

My mom hugged me and whispered, "Good luck." And Isa gave me our secret Team P sign from when we were little—two thumbs-up but with the thumbs touching each other. I smiled.

"Be your sunshiny self," Isa said. "It's your best quality."

I followed the small group of people who'd been called along with me, and we were led into an auditorium. The judges all sat in the front row, while the singers lined up along the stairs at stage left and took turns going center stage, where the microphone was.

At least I've used a microphone before, I thought. *I'm ready for this!*

I was able to watch numbers eighty through eighty-three go before me. Number eighty was good but not particularly amazing. Eighty-one was very anxious, and he kept wiping his hands on his pants. I made a mental note not to do that myself.

Eighty-two couldn't carry a tune, and eighty-three was very, very good. I almost wished I hadn't listened to her. She had to be at least sixteen and was very poised, with a beautiful green print dress and bright pink fingernails. It was a good thing that I wasn't able to see the judges' reactions when she sang—I think that would have made me even more nervous.

"Number eighty-four!" one of the judges called.

I walked slowly up the steps and to the center of the stage. There were two women and one man sitting with clipboards and pencils, staring at me expectantly.

"What is your name and age?" asked the woman with brown hair.

I gulped. This was it. Time to turn on my sunshine and win over these judges. I could do it! I would just pretend I was working at the register at Molly's and trying to win over a grumpy customer with my charm.

"Hello!" I said boldly. "I'm Sierra Perez, and I'm thirteen years old. I'm in eighth grade at MLK Middle School, and I'm very glad to be here."

The male judge smiled back. In fact, all three of them smiled and looked a bit more jolly. "Great to have you, Sierra. What will you be singing for us today?"

"I'll be singing an original song called 'Be Yourself.' It was written by my band, the Wildflowers. We're all eighth graders, and we perform a mix of covers and original songs."

"Very impressive," said one of the women judges. "And I love original songs. They keep things interesting."

"Begin whenever you're ready," said the man.

I nodded and took two deep breaths. I even shook out my arms and legs for a second, which is something I do right before I perform with the Wildflowers. It's like I'm wiggling the nerves out so I can do my best.

Then I cleared my throat and began to sing.

"Be yourself! Who's better than you?
Be yourself! You're the only one who
Knows what you like,
Knows who you love,
Knows all your dreams and your secret
wishes too.
You don't depend on anyone else because
you need to
Just—be yourself!"

It was going great. My voice sounded strong, even though I hadn't warmed up much, and I made sure to keep a smile in my voice.

But then, as I was about to start the second verse, something awful happened. *I forgot the rest of the words.*

I stood there, frozen onstage, my mouth slightly open. I quickly smiled and acted as if this were just a natural pause in the song. After all, it was an original and the judges didn't know it. But I'm sure they could see the panic in my eyes.

Then, out of nowhere, I remembered what the tour guide at the ice cream factory had said. *Anything that goes wrong while you're creating art can be turned into something* beautiful. . . . Just beautiful-oops it!

I took a deep breath and started singing again. This time, though, I made up the words as I went along.

> *"Be yourself! Make a mistake and plow*
> *right through it!*
> *Be yourself! Betcha no one even knew it!*
> *Hmmmm mmm mmm mmm.*
> *Just. . . . Be. . . . Yourself!"*

When I was done, I gave the judges another huge smile and a bow. I acted as if I had planned for the song to go exactly as I'd sung it, and that I hadn't improvised and made up the second verse.

I had beautiful-oops'd it.

The judges were all writing and taking notes. One of them, the lady with the brown hair, smiled and said, "That was very nice, Sierra. You forgot the words for a moment there, didn't you?"

Uh-oh. I guess I hadn't pulled it off quite as well

as I'd hoped. I knew it was best to be honest.

I nodded. "Yes, I did," I admitted. "And I know the song! I think I was just so nervous about the audition. I'm sorry."

"Don't be sorry," said the other female judge. "I thought you handled it beautifully. You recovered very well."

"Thank you," I said. I kept the smile on my face, but inside I was kicking myself. There was no way someone who'd forgotten the words to their song was going to win! If I had just picked my song sooner, I could have practiced it more and known the words without even thinking about them.

Instead I would have to go back to the waiting room and tell Mami, Isa, Allie, and Tamiko that I had botched my big break.

Even worse, I'd have to tell the Wildflowers that I'd messed up one of our original songs! I couldn't believe it. I bowed again, stiffly, and walked offstage and back to the waiting room, where everyone was supposed to stay until the end, when they announced the finalists.

And just like that, the audition was over. Instead of feeling relief, I just felt mad at myself. Yes, I had made the best of it with my beautiful oops, but I hadn't been able to show the judges my very best singing or performance. And it was my own fault.

After so much buildup, my performance had been very, very disappointing, and there was no way to put a sprinkle of happy on that.

CHAPTER TEN
MELTED DREAMS

There was nothing left to do but wait.

I walked down the long hallway back to the waiting area and saw Allie, Tamiko, Isa, and my mother looking anxious. When I walked in, they all jumped up and down and clapped and congratulated me.

"Don't congratulate me," I said mournfully. "I messed up—big-time."

"What do you mean?" asked Allie. "What happened?"

"I choked."

"Literally?" asked Isa.

"Not, not *literally*. I performance-choked."

I explained to them how I'd started out smiling and happy and cheerful, and that the judges had seemed to like me. Then I'd started my song and completely blown it. I'd taken a long pause and then made up the second verse out of thin air.

When I was finished explaining the whole sad story to them, my mom gave me a huge hug, and everyone else piled on as well, until I was the center of a five-person hug. Everyone around us probably thought we were a little odd, but I didn't care. I was upset and disappointed in myself, and I needed my friends and family.

"Thanks, guys," I said. "It means a lot."

"At least you managed to beautiful-oops it!" said Tamiko. "I bet that impressed the judges a lot."

"I guess so," I said glumly.

"It impresses *me*," she added with a smile.

"I just have this feeling that you'll make the finals anyway," said Allie. "So you forgot the words for a second. So what? It happens! Probably ten people did that."

"Yeah, you can charm anyone, Sierra," said Tamiko. "I know you'll make it to the finals."

Isa was weirdly quiet. I knew that her twin-tuition was telling her how angry I was at myself, and she was feeling that pain like it was her own. That was the way it was with identical twins, even when they weren't very identical in personality.

The next two hours passed slowly. My mom went out and brought us back some snacks, and all of us sat and started our homework while we waited. I couldn't believe how long we'd been there, and I started to feel terrible that my friends were sitting there waiting with me for hours on a school night.

"Tell your parents to pick you up!" I told them. "My mom and Isa are here. You don't have to stay."

I didn't say what I was worried about, which was that, with the way they'd been acting lately, I didn't want them thinking I was some queen bee who expected them to spend an entire afternoon hanging around in a waiting room. I knew in my gut that my chances were slim, and getting the bad news after making everyone wait here with me for hours would just make me feel even worse.

"*Of course* we're staying," said Allie. "Don't be silly."

It felt like another hour went by, but it was probably only twenty minutes later when the judges finally came into the room.

The lady with the brown hair had a microphone, and she said, "Thank you all for coming out today to audition. Thank you also for your patience as we watched each contestant perform and took the time to give everyone careful consideration. We are very impressed with the talent here! You all have bright futures ahead of you."

Everyone clapped politely, but quickly, as we all just wanted to get on to the part where they told us who the finalists were.

The lady passed the microphone to the male judge. He said, "And now we'll announce our ten finalists, who will all appear on the show in a few weeks. Without further ado, our first finalist is . . . Alicia Freed!"

It was the girl in the green print dress who'd gone right before me. I watched her jump up and down and go up to the front of the room to stand by the judges. Her face was as pink as her nails, and she looked so, so happy.

I felt my stomach twist. I wanted to be up there so badly! And what were the chances that they'd pick me, when I'd performed right after Alicia and forgotten the words?

They called the other finalists' names one by one. Allie and Tamiko each held one of my hands, and they took turns squeezing my hand for support every time my name wasn't called.

Finally it was time for finalist number ten.

"And our last finalist is . . . Phillip Lum!"

Phillip ran excitedly to the front of the room. I counted and recounted all of the finalists and had to accept that my name had not been called. I was not in the top ten.

I knew it had been a long shot, but I felt just as disappointed as I would have if I'd had an amazing audition. I had really thought my singing ability was something special and that if I just had a chance to show it to the judges, they'd notice me.

My mother and my friends sat in stunned silence for a moment. No one knew what to say, least of all me. But I had to break the silence.

"Oh well. It was a good experience, right?" I said, trying for the old Sierra charm. "After all, it was fun to come and see all the contestants. And to try something different . . ."

"Let's get out of here," said Tamiko. "These judges don't know anything about talent."

Isa was still silent, and my mom gave me another hug. I felt terrible, and also, slightly embarrassed. Had

I really expected to make it to the finals in such a big, talented group of kids, most of whom were older and more experienced than I was? Now it seemed laughable that I was even here.

"Let's go," my mom said. "I'll drive everyone home."

The car was quiet on the way back to Bayville. I felt like I had let everyone down, even Isa, who had been so proud of me.

Maybe I didn't have what it took to be a star after all. It was a sad feeling.

It seemed like my dad had gotten home just before we did. He was washing his hands at the kitchen sink when we walked in. He looked hopeful and expectant, which meant that my mom had not texted him. So I had to break the bad news to him as well. It was hard to tell him that I hadn't made it, especially after he and my mom had warned me from the beginning that there would be many people trying out and it would be a very competitive process.

"It doesn't matter, Sierra," he said. "It was a good experience!"

I nodded mutely. Then the four of us worked

together to get dinner onto the table, and we sat down to reheated ropa vieja leftovers.

My parents kept up a steady stream of chitchat to distract me, but Isa had been eerily silent since we'd gotten the news from the judges. I don't think she had opened her mouth a single time in the car on the way home except to mutter good-bye to Allie and Tamiko.

When there was a break in my parents' overly cheery conversation, I said, "What's up, Isa? You haven't said a word."

Isa looked down at her food, which she was pushing around on her plate.

"Are you disappointed in me?" I asked. "Did I let Team Perez down?" My tone was teasing, trying to make light of a bad situation, but deep down I was pretty sure that that was how she felt.

Isa looked up at me, her eyes wide. "Seriously? That's what you think?"

"I don't know what to think," I said slowly. "I'm so mad at myself! I really blew it. And after everyone in my band and my friends and you all helped me and encouraged me. I thought I could be a star, and instead I'm just . . . well, just number eighty-four."

"You're *not* just number eighty-four," Isa said hotly. "You did something really brave, Sisi. You tried out! You showed up and stood in front of those judges and the other kids in your group and you sang. And then you messed up—and you *didn't* run offstage crying! You pulled it together and you kept on going. I'm really proud." Her voice broke a bit, as if she were overwhelmed by emotion. "I can't even . . ."

She didn't finish her sentence, just looked back down at her food. My parents exchanged looks with each other, and then with me, trying to figure out what was going on.

But I was pretty sure I knew. The way Isa had looked at the other contestants lining up when we'd been at the audition, almost hungrily, as if she'd wanted to join them. She was a competitive person. I'd watched her play soccer many times, and she was as aggressive as anyone else I'd ever seen. When her team lost, she sometimes kicked her water bottle or threw her jersey.

"You wish you'd tried out too," I said softly. And it wasn't twin-tuition that told me that. It was the look on her face.

Isa nodded, as my parents' expressions grew more and more confused.

"Isa! Why on Earth would you want to try out?" Papi asked.

"You don't even sing," said Mami.

Isa didn't reply. I had a feeling, though, that she wouldn't mind now if I explained for her. It seemed like she wanted to talk about it.

"Isa has been taking singing lessons," I blurted out.

You could have knocked my parents over with a feather. They both looked at Isa, their forks paused halfway between their mouths and their plates.

Isa's face turned red.

"Isa? Is this true?" asked my mom.

Isa nodded. "Yes. I've been taking them at Middle C and paying for them myself. I, um, really like singing too."

"Since when?" asked my dad. "Why didn't you tell us?"

Isa shrugged. "I don't know why. It started by accident, I guess. I was just always singing to myself when I listened to music. But then I started liking it more and more, and I thought about joining the choir at school, but everyone would be so surprised if I did that. . . ."

Isa didn't mention that her usual attitude of quiet, surly grumpiness and her refusal to join anything at school was pretty well known. She was right—it would have seemed really out of character for her to suddenly join the choir, and she would not have wanted all that attention.

"Anyway, I'm not trying to be like Sierra." Here she paused and looked at me pointedly. "She has her band, and that's *her thing*. I just like to sing and would like to get better at it. That's all."

Mami's face broke into a huge grin. "Well! How lucky are we to have TWO musical daughters in the family!"

"Very lucky," echoed Papi. "And I am so proud of you both. Sierra, I'm proud of you for trying out today, and doing something truly courageous. You are a talented girl, and if you continue to work hard, good things will happen! I promise. And, Isa, I am proud of you for following your passion, because I can tell you have been beating yourself up about it. Don't! Never be afraid to be who you are."

Isa laughed loudly. "Papi, are you telling me to *be myself*?"

"Be yourself!" I sang. "Who's better than you? Be yourself! You're the only one who . . ."

And then Isa jumped in and sang along with me.

"Knows what you like!
Knows who you love!
Knows all your dreams and your secret
wishes too.
You don't depend on anyone else because
you need to
Just . . . beeeeee yourrrrselllllf!"

Our parents burst into applause, and Isa and I stood up and took a bow together. "Team Perez," I said, grabbing Isa's hand.

"Team Perez," she repeated.

CHAPTER ELEVEN

TUNE IN TONIGHT

It was a huge relief that I hadn't told anyone else at school about the audition except for MacKenzie. She and Tamiko were incredibly nice and sympathetic at school Friday morning, while also understanding that I did *not* want to talk about it, and I particularly did not want anyone else to find out about it.

I made it through the school day focusing on my schoolwork and teachers and trying to be my normal, cheerful self. But inside, I couldn't wait for the bell to ring and for it to be the weekend.

I let myself sleep in on Saturday morning, which I rarely do, because usually I'm off to a soccer game, or a lighting rehearsal for the school play, or a band practice. But today was one of those magical

Saturdays when I didn't have any obligations. I stayed in my pajamas and read a book in bed for a while. Then, when I finally got up, I made myself some tea and toast and sat in the kitchen watching TV on the tiny set in the corner. The next day I had to work at Molly's, but today I could just *relax*.

The house phone rang while I was cleaning up my dishes. I waited to see if one of my parents would get it, since the home line meant it was probably one of the vet techs from their clinic calling or one of my grandparents. But after three rings no one had answered it, so I picked up.

"Hello?"

"Hello! May I speak to Sierra Perez, please?"

It was a woman's voice that I didn't recognize. Definitely not the clinic or one of my grandparents.

Something in her tone sounded extremely professional and important. I cleared my throat before answering, "Yes, this is Sierra. Who's calling, please?"

"Sierra, this is Cynthia Meadows. I was one of the judges at the Who's a Star? contest. I'm not sure if you remember me. . . . I was wearing a navy-blue jacket."

Did I remember her? Of *course* I remembered

her! It was my first-ever audition for a TV singing program, and there had been only three judges. The question was, why was she calling *me*?

"Yes, I remember you, Ms. Meadows," I said. "How are you?"

"I'm well, thank you," she replied. "I'm calling because I happened to see your face after we announced the finalists, and I saw how disappointed you were."

I felt my cheeks flush. She was calling because I'd looked so pitiful? That wasn't exactly flattering.

"Um, yes, I suppose I was," I admitted. "Not that I'd had expectations or anything. I was just, you know, hopeful. But I'm okay, Ms. Meadows. You didn't have to call—"

Ms. Meadows cut in. "I know I didn't have to. I wanted to, Sierra. For several reasons. One, I want to make sure you turn on your TV tonight and watch the promotion for the show, which will be airing at eight o'clock. And two, I wanted to have the chance to tell you privately that I think you have a beautiful voice."

I gulped. She thought my voice was beautiful? I felt my insides turn to goo. "Really?"

"Really," she said. "Your voice is terrific. The other judges agreed. We just felt that you need more time to work on your composure. You were so nervous, which is natural, of course, and you are very young. But the more you sing, the more relaxed you'll become."

"Yes, of course," I said. "I plan to keep singing! Don't worry about that."

"Good. Because I also wanted to say that I hope you continue to work on your music and take it seriously. And I hope you'll consider trying out for the Who's a Star? contest again next year. We had so many contestants come out in the Hamilton-Bayville area that it seems clear this will become an annual thing!"

They were going to do contest tryouts here again! I would have another chance. It was the best news in the world!

"Thank you, Ms. Meadows. That means so much to me. I will definitely try out again next year! Wild horses couldn't stop me."

Ms. Meadows laughed. "I'm glad to hear it. Now don't forget—watch the show's promotion tonight at eight o'clock. And you might want to tell your friends and family to watch too. All right?"

"Yes, I will. I'll tell everyone, *and* I'll be cheering for all of those finalists. Thanks again for calling!"

I hung up the phone, feeling significantly more cheerful than I'd been when I'd picked it up. Ms. Meadows had called me personally to tell me to keep singing. Me! Maybe I wasn't a star yet, but that didn't mean it couldn't happen someday.

I couldn't help but wonder, though, why she'd asked me to watch the promo for a show I wouldn't be on. Would it have details for next year's contest? Or did she just want a lot of people to tune in and drive up ratings? I hoped it wasn't the last reason. I grabbed my phone to text Allie and Tamiko. For half a second I thought about *not* telling them because of their weird up-and-down behavior toward me lately. But they'd been so supportive at the audition the other day, and they were my best friends. I wanted them to know. I started typing.

Hey! One of the judges from the contest called me and told me to watch the promo for the show tonight at 8pm. She told me to tell my friends to watch too! So, you know, WATCH!

Allie wrote back immediately. She called you personally? Sierra, that's amazing! Of course I'll watch.

A few minutes later, Tamiko sent me the thumbs-up emoji and Can't wait for 8!

Next I texted my bandmates. I had given them a very brief summary of how my audition had gone, not wanting to make too big a deal out of my beautiful-oops moment, especially since Tessa was the one who had written the words to the song.

We'll ALL be watching, Reagan promised. Want to come over and the whole band can watch from my garage?

I'm not on the show! I reminded her. It's probably just info about next year. I just wanted to tell you guys because you're the best bandmates ever and the judge told me to spread the word. Thanks for all of your help preparing!

And lastly, when my parents got home from the clinic later that afternoon, I told them and Isa that we had to watch the promo that night after dinner.

"Of course," said Papi. "I want to know all about this contest! I think it's great news that they'll be doing it again. You have a whole year to practice."

"I don't understand why she'd call you to tell you to watch a promo for a show you're not on," Isa grumbled. "That just seems mean to me."

"She didn't," I said. "She called to tell me to keep working on my singing, and that there would be another contest next year, *and* that I should watch the promo."

I was defending Ms. Meadows because she had been so nice and complimentary on the phone, but the truth was, I had no idea why I was telling everyone to watch the promo either.

"Who cares?" said my mom. "I would watch it anyway just because I'm curious about how this contest will work, and I want to see the kids who were finalists. I'm very proud of every single kid there who tried out."

My mom's tone was so matter-of-fact that the discussion ended there, and turned to the chocolate Labrador retriever my dad had examined earlier in the day who had eaten a mango pit.

After dinner Isa, my parents, and I cleaned up the kitchen and headed into the family room to hang out while we waited for the promo to come on. I felt jumpy and excited inside, even though I didn't have any idea what there was to be jumpy and excited about.

Then the texts started coming in.

I've got my TV on, texted Reagan. Remind me why we're watching?

Ready to watch! said Allie. Did you make it onto the show and tell us you didn't, just to have a big reveal? Those shows LOVE a big reveal!

No reveal ☹️☹️, I texted back. And, I have no idea why we're watching!

"Stop texting, Sierra!" said my mom. "Look, here it is!" She grabbed the remote, turned the volume up, and looked at the screen intently.

The promo started with a shot of the outside of the community center. The camera panned on the line of kids outside waiting to go in. Before I could even see if I was in that line, the promo switched to another shot of everyone in the waiting room, holding their numbers and warming up their voices.

"It was our biggest crowd ever for a Who's a Star? audition!" said the announcer. "So many amazing young singers turned out for this audition. We'll definitely be returning to the Hamilton–Bayville area next year!"

Then the view switched to a shot of a boy trying out. It was the one with the deep, raspy voice who'd been ahead of me in line.

"Hey! I remember him," said Isa. "I can't believe he didn't make it. He was really good."

"They were all good," said my mom, looking over at me hastily, as if she were worried that seeing the promo would get me upset again about not having made the show. But I wasn't upset. It was fun to watch, and I actually felt a little proud. I had been a part of this!

Then, suddenly—there I was. On *television*.

"SIERRA, THAT'S YOU!" shouted Isa, who ran up to the TV to get closer, blocking our view.

"Move, Isa!" my dad said.

My jaw dropped as I stared at myself on the screen, singing.

> *"Be yourself! Who's better than you?*
> *Be yourself! You're the only one who . . ."*

It was the beginning of the song, and I sounded pretty good! I felt myself puff up slightly with pride. I *had* done okay in the beginning. Then, just before I blanked on the words, the scene cut to the judges discussing me.

The male judge said, "I don't think this young lady is ready for the show just yet."

"I agree, but it would be great to see her again when she's older," said the second woman judge.

Then Ms. Meadows said, "For sure. She has a

special quality." She looked down at her clipboard and wrote something. Then she turned to the other judges and said, "Sierra Perez. Remember that name. She could be a star someday."

The promo then cut to another kid's audition.

There was a ringing in my ears, and I was so happy that I almost felt faint.

She could be a star someday. She'd said that about *me*!

"That was you!" Isa yelled, jumping up and down. No one was paying attention to the rest of the promo anymore. "That was you, Sisi!"

My parents were both red-faced and smiling. They hugged me and hugged me again. "Our daughter! We are so proud of you!"

My phone started lighting up with text message after text message.

Ah!!!!!!!!!!!!!!!!!!! Tamiko wrote.

Allie's text was more eloquent but just as enthusiastic: FUTURE STAR SIERRA PEREZ!

The Wildflowers group text also exploded. And I could see that I was getting messages from classmates and club mates that hadn't known I had auditioned.

I looked up from my phone, a little teary-eyed, and smiled at my family. "I couldn't have done it without all of you," I said. "My family and my friends and my bandmates."

I looked at Isa, who had an uncharacteristically large grin on her face. "Especially you, Isa," I continued. "You helped me so much, getting ready for the audition. Maybe Team P will sing together someday. What do you think?"

"Really?" she asked.

I nodded. "Really."

Isa grinned. "Well, we do have a lot of talent in this family. Two veterinarians . . . Why not two singers? Team P can do anything they set their minds to!"

CHAPTER TWELVE
STAR POWER

On Sunday, I was excited to get to Molly's. I always looked forward to going to work, because my job was scooping ice cream with my friends, but today I was extra excited, because I was still tingling about the fact that Ms. Meadows had said I had what it took to be a star.

Maybe it wouldn't happen for a long time, and maybe it wouldn't happen *ever*, but the fact that a talent judge had said that about me meant the world.

I skipped through the door of the ice cream shop a full sixteen minutes early, which was practically unheard of for me. Allie was already there, of course, since she always came early with her mom or got dropped off by her dad if she was staying at his apartment.

"Yay! It's Sierra—my only fa[...] been on TV," teased Allie.

I took a huge bow and pretended t[...] grand and fancy. Then I checked the trash cans[...] of my regular tasks—and saw that they were near[...] filled to the top.

"This TV star is going to take the trash out," I said. "I'll be back after this commercial break."

Allie giggled and got her chalk out, ready to put up the day's book and ice cream pairing. The specials board was blank again.

We were really letting Mrs. Shear down. I resolved to spend today's entire shift thinking of the perfect new ice cream special. I owed a lot to Molly's. Not only was serving ice cream a great job, but Molly's was a fun, happy place to work, and I got an automatic date every single week with my two best friends, one of whom I probably wouldn't see very often because she now lived one town away.

Molly's was a huge part of my life.

When I came back inside from the dumpster, Tamiko had arrived and was putting on her apron. She clapped when she saw me and gave me a huge hug. "I knew you could it," she said. "I just knew it!"

I still didn't make the

now. But you made a
...ced Sierra Perez to the
well!"

o. That means a lot."

...kled, and an older couple
d to be their grandson. It
was time to g...

"Hello!" Tamiko said cheerfully. "Welcome to Molly's. What can I get for you today? We have some very special Mint Lemonade ice cream this week, and one of our most popular flavors, Honey Lavender!"

"Mmm-mmm," said the woman. "I'd like a double-scoop sugar cone of the Honey Lavender, please."

"And how about you, Mitchell?" the man asked the little boy. "What do you want?"

"Brownies," he mumbled. "I want *brownies*."

Uh-oh. This was going to be tough.

"I'm afraid we don't have any brownies today. How about I make you a black-and-white milk-shake?" Tamiko suggested.

The boy shook his head at Tamiko, disgusted. He wanted *brownies*.

Then the man stared at me. He squinted his eyes. He elbowed his wife and whispered something into her ear.

Self-consciously I tucked my hair behind my ears and smoothed my apron. Had I forgotten to wash my face or something? Was there food in my teeth? A huge stain on my shirt that I couldn't see?

"You're that girl!" said the man finally. "From the Who's a Star? contest. We watched the commercial for it last night and we heard you sing. You were great!"

I blushed furiously. It was one thing to have my friends and family know about it, but to be recognized by a stranger was very different. He'd seen me on TV!

"You were terrific," the woman said. "And I can't wait to watch the show when it comes on in a week or two. I just love those singing competitions."

I looked at Allie and Tamiko for help, partly because I was embarrassed and partly so that they would see that I wasn't taking this too seriously.

But they were exchanging a look between them—just like the looks I'd seen before at the ice cream factory tour. I felt flustered all over again.

"Thank you! Um, how about trying our Cocoa

Coconuts flavor?" I suggested. "It's really chocolaty, just like a brownie. But it's even more fun."

The man nodded. "Sounds perfect. We'll get two single cups of your Cocoa Coconuts, please. And sign our cups . . . if you wouldn't mind."

"Coming right up!" said Allie. "Sierra, you sign first, then hand me the cup to scoop, please."

I felt myself blushing even more as I took a marker from the drawer under the counter and signed my name on their ice cream cups. No one had ever asked for my autograph before. I wondered if it would ever happen again.

I handed the cups to Allie, who set to work scooping. Tamiko stood quietly, which was unusual for her.

When the customers left and we were alone again in the shop, I whirled around to face Allie and Tamiko.

"Okay, guys. Spill it," I said. "What is with all the looks between the two of you? Do you think I'm getting a big ego or something? I'm not! I promise. In fact, I was crushed last week after the audition. It really shook my self-confidence. But then, after Ms. Meadows's call, I started to feel better. And seeing the promo helped. But I don't want you thinking that I think I'm so great or something. Because I *don't*, okay?"

"But you *are* great," said Allie. "That's what Tamiko and I think! You've always had that special, bubbly Sierra charm. And that's what we called it—your charm! But I think Ms. Meadows was right. You're a star in the making. It's your star power."

Tamiko, who looked like the cat that ate the canary, pulled out a piece of chalk and walked over to the specials board. "The reason you've noticed us exchanging 'looks' as you called them is because Allie and I came up with the *perfect* new special for Molly's two weeks ago. It's called the Sierra Sundae! We didn't want to tell you about it, because we wanted to save it as a celebration after you won the Who's a Star? tryouts."

"A Sierra Sundae?" I repeated, shocked.

"We thought you'd win for sure, because we had no idea how many people would try out . . . ," Allie said hesitantly.

Then Tamiko jumped back in. "And then we were worried when you *didn't* make it, because we didn't want the idea for the special sundae to hurt your feelings. . . ."

Tamiko and Allie both paused and looked at me. I was so floored, it took me a second to realize that they were worried I wouldn't like the idea. "I love it! I'm just really surprised! Thank you!" I said, beaming at my BFFs.

"Good! Now that you were on TV and that lady said all those nice things about you, it's perfect!" Allie jumped up and down and squealed. "I'm going to make a Sierra Sundae now to put out on social media."

Tamiko reached up with her chalk and wrote, "Who's a Star? Ask about our new Sierra Sundae!" on the board, using her beautiful, curly handwriting and adding tons of little yellow stars.

I couldn't believe it. I had been stressing out about my friends' looks, and about not having an idea to present to Mrs. Shear. But the big secret my friends had been keeping from me was that they'd come up with an ice cream special—*about me*! Allie was scooping and shaping and working her magic, and Tamiko put on some music. When Allie was done, she handed me an absolutely beautiful creation—it was a sundae with a star-shaped cookie on top, and plenty of our signature sprinkles.

"The ice cream flavor is Star Anise, because we think you're a star!" Allie said.

"We're so proud of you," Tamiko added.

I had tears in my eyes, and I knew I had to record this moment. I took a picture of the sundae and sent it to my parents and Isa and my bandmates. Then I grabbed an eraser and Tamiko's chalk and rewrote what she'd written on the board.

"Each and every one of us is a star! Try our new Star Sundae today and reach for your dreams!"

"That's perfect," said Allie. "I love it!"

"It's amazing. Maybe you should be the marketing person instead of me, Sierra," Tamiko joked.

Then Tamiko took one of her fancy pictures of the sundae, using all the special photo filters, and posted it on Molly's social media accounts, with the blurb We are all STARS! Come try our new Star Sundae!

Business started to pick up then, and some of our regular customers came in. A few had seen the promo for the singing contest and congratulated me. And then, just when the line we'd had for more than a half hour was starting to get under control, my parents and Isa came in, followed by the rest of the Wildflowers.

"Sierra!" my bandmates yelled. "You're a star!"

"Anyone can be a star here at Molly's," I said. "Just try our new Star Sundae!"

Everyone in my family ordered the new special, and so did Kasey and Tessa from my band. But Reagan said she didn't like the taste of star anise.

"It tastes like licorice, which I also don't like," she said. "But I'm in the mood for some plain old vanilla. I'd like a double scoop of that, please."

"Coming right up!" said Allie. "We don't keep it out here in the case, because it's not as popular as our more unusual flavors. But we have some in the back."

Allie disappeared backstage while I waited on new customers and chatted with my family and friends. It was turning out to be one of the best days at work I'd ever had.

It was funny how things worked out sometimes. I had thought that the only positive outcome of auditioning for the singing contest would be to make it onto the show and be a finalist. But instead the contest had brought me much closer to my twin sister, shown me how much my friends cared about me, and given me the confidence in my abilities to keep singing, knowing that maybe I *did* have a future in music someday.

And I'd gotten all of that from a contest that *hadn't* picked me! Life was pretty amazing sometimes.

"*Psst . . .* Sierra."

Allie was whispering at me from the doorway to the back of Molly's. By the look on her face, I could tell that something was wrong.

I walked over to her and said quietly, "What is it?"

"We're out of vanilla! I can't believe it. Mom used it up yesterday when she was trying out a new flavor. You know how I hate telling a customer we're out of something . . . especially vanilla!"

Allie looked mortified. We had all these customers in the store, and they would hear her tell Reagan that we didn't have a basic flavor. Mrs. Shear would be disappointed too. She liked every customer to be 100 percent happy when they left her store.

Tamiko looked over at us urgently from the cash register. That was normally my job, so I could tell she was stressed and unhappy that I'd left her there. Her eyes said, *Hurry back, please!*

"There's only one thing you can do," I told Allie. "You're going to have to beautiful-oops it! Make her a double scoop of the Elderberry Flower, and put a load of crazy toppings on it, and call it our other new special . . . the Wildflower!"

Allie's face broke into a huge smile. "Right! Of

course! I'll beautiful-oops it, just like you did the other day. Great idea!"

Allie got to work, and when she handed the cone to Reagan, she said, "I know you asked for vanilla, but this is a custom cone just for you. It's called the Wildflower!"

Reagan's face lit up like a sky full of fireworks. There really is something magical about ice cream. Just the right flavor can change your day from a good one to a spectacular one. And it has the power to keep friendships going strong.

"Don't forget your sprinkle of happy," I said, adding some multicolored sprinkles to her cone.

It was such a nice afternoon that everyone stayed and ate at the tables outside or milled around inside the store, talking. Allie, Tamiko, and I were busy, but so happy to be together with our friends and family there.

"I think Molly's is my favorite place in the world," said Allie, sighing with contentment.

"Me too," said Tamiko.

"Me three," I agreed. "Sprinkle Sundays sisters forever!"

Still Hungry?
Here's a taste of the first book in the

series, *Hole in the Middle*.

Donuts Are My Life

My grandmother started Donut Dreams, a little counter in my family's restaurant that sells her now-famous homemade donuts, when my dad was about my age. The name was inspired by my grandmother's dream to save enough money from the business to send him to any college he wanted, even if it was far away from our small town.

It worked. Well, it kind of worked. I mean, my grandmother's donuts are pretty legendary. Her counter is so successful that instead of only selling donuts in the morning, the shop is now open all day. Her donuts have even won all sorts of awards, and there are rumors that there's a cooking show on TV that might come film a segment about how she started Donut Dreams from virtually nothing.

My grandmother, whom I call Nans—short for Nana—raised enough money to send my dad to college out of state all the way in Chicago. But then he came back. I've heard Nans was happy about that, but I'm not because it means I'm stuck here in this small town.

So now it's my turn to come up with my own "donut dreams," because I am dreaming about going to college in a big, glamorous city somewhere far, far away. Dad jokes that if I do go to Chicago, I have to come back like he did.

No way, I thought to myself. Nobody ever moves here, and nobody ever seems to move away, either. It's just the same old, same old, every year: the Fall Fling, the Halloween Hoot Fair, Thanksgiving, Snowflake Festival, New Year's, Valentine's Day and the Sweetheart Ball . . . I mean, we know what's coming.

Everyone makes a big deal about the first day of school, but it's not like you're with new kids or anything. There's one elementary school, one middle school, and one high school.

Our grandparents used to go to a regional school, which meant they were with kids from other towns in high school. But the school was about forty-five minutes away, and getting there and back was a big pain, so they eventually decided to keep everyone at the high school here. It's a big old building where my dad went to school, and his brother and my aunt, and just about everyone else's parents.

Some kids do go away for college. My BFF Casey's sister, Gabby, is one of them. She keeps telling Casey that she should go to the same college so they can live together while Gabby goes to medical school, which is her dream. It's a cool idea, but what's the point of moving away from everything if you just end up moving in with your sister?

Maybe it's that I don't have a sister, I have a brother, and living with him is messy. I mean that literally. Skylar is ten. He spits globs of toothpaste in the sink, his clothes are all over his room, and he drinks milk directly from the carton, which makes Nans shriek.

My grandparents basically live with us now, which is a whole long story. Well, the short story is that my mother died two years ago. After Mom died, everyone was a mess, so Nans and Grandpa ended up helping out a lot. Their house is only a short drive down the street from us, so it makes sense they're around all the time.

Even their dog comes over now, which is good because I love him, but weird because Mom would never let us get a pet. I still feel like she's going to come walking in the door one day and be really mad that there's a dog running around with muddy paws.

My mother was an artist. She was an art teacher in the middle school where I'm starting this year, which will be kind of weird.

There's a big mural that all her students painted on one wall of the school after she died. The last time I was in the school was when they had a ceremony and put a plaque next to it with her name on it. Now I'll see it every day.

It's not like I don't think about her every day anyway. Her studio is still set up downstairs. It's a small room off the kitchen with great light. For a while none of us went in there, or we'd just kind of tiptoe in and see if we could still smell her.

Lately we use it more. I like to go in and sit in her favorite chair and read. It's a cozy chair with lots of pillows you can kind of sink into, and I like to think it's her giving me a hug. Dad uses her big worktable to do paperwork. The only people who don't go in are Nans and Grandpa. Dad grumbles that it's the one room in the house that Nans hasn't invaded.

Sometimes I catch Nans in the doorway, though, just looking at Mom's paintings on the walls. Mom liked to paint pictures of us and flowers. One wall is covered in black-and-white sketches of us and the other is this really cool, colorful collection of painted flowers with some close up, some far away, and some in vases. I could stare at them for hours.

I remember there used to be fresh flowers all over the house. Mom even had little vases with flowers in the bathrooms, which was a little crazy, especially since Skylar always knocked them over and there would be puddles of water everywhere.

Sometimes when I had a bad day she'd make a special little arrangement for me and put it next to my bed. When she was sick, I used to go out to her garden and cut them and make little bouquets for her.

I'd put them on her night table, just like she did for me. Nans always makes sure there are flowers on the kitchen table, but it's not really the same.

Grandpa and Nans own a restaurant called the Park View Table. Locals call it the Park for short. They don't get any points for originality, because the restaurant is literally across from a park, so it has a park view. But it seems to be the place in town where everyone ends up.

On the weekends everyone stops by in the mornings, either to pick up donuts and coffee or for these giant pancakes that everyone loves. Lunch is busy during the week, with everyone on their lunch breaks and some older people who meet there regularly, and dinnertime is the slowest. I know all this because I basically grew up there.

Nans comes up with the menus and the specials, and she's always trying out new recipes with the chef. Or on us. Luckily, Nans is a great cook, but some of her "creative" dishes are a little too kooky to eat.

Nans still makes a lot of the donuts, but Dad does too, especially the creative ones. Donut Dreams used to have just the usual sugar or jelly-filled or chocolate, which were all delicious, but Dad started making

PB&J donuts and banana crème donuts.

At first people laughed, but then they started to try them. Word of mouth made the donuts popular, and for a little while, people were confused because they didn't realize Donut Dreams was a counter inside the Park. They instead kept looking for a donut shop.

My uncle Charlie gives my dad a hard time sometimes, teasing him that he's the "big-city boy with the fancy ideas." Uncle Charlie loves my dad, and my dad loves him, but I sometimes wonder if Uncle Charlie and Aunt Melissa are a little mad that Dad got to go away to school and they went to the state school nearby.

My dad runs Donut Dreams. Uncle Charlie does all the ordering for food and napkins and everything you need in a restaurant, and Aunt Melissa is the accountant who manages all the financial stuff, like the payroll and paying all the bills. So between my dad, his brother, and his sister, and the cousins working at the restaurant, it's a lot of family, all the time.

My brother, Skylar, and I are the youngest of seven cousins. I like having cousins, but some of them think they can tell me what to do, and that's five extra people bossing me around.

"There's room for everyone in the Park!" Grandpa likes to say when he sees us all running around, but honestly, sometimes the Park feels pretty crowded.

That's the thing: in a small town, I always feel like there are too many people. Maybe it's just that there are too many people I know, or who know me.

Right after Mom died I couldn't go anywhere without someone coming up to me and putting an arm around me or patting me on the head. People were nice, don't get me wrong, but everyone knows everything in a small town. Sometimes I feel like I can't breathe.

Mom grew up outside of Chicago, and that's where my other grandmother, her mother, still lives. I call her Mimi. We go there every Thanksgiving, which I love. I remember asking her once when we were at the supermarket why there were so many people she didn't know. She laughed and explained that she lived in a big town, where most people don't know each other.

It fascinated me that she could walk into the supermarket and no one there would know where she had just been, or that she bought a store-bought cake and was going to tell everyone she baked it. No one was peering into her cart and asking what she was making for lunch, or how the tomatoes tasted last week. Nans always wonders if Mimi is lonely, since she lives by herself, but it sounds nice to me.

Everyone in our family pitches in, but I officially start working at Donut Dreams next week for a full shift every day, which is kind of nice. I'll work for Dad. He bought me a T-shirt that says THE DREAM TEAM that I can wear when I'm behind the counter.

We have a couple of really small tables near the counter that are separate from the restaurant, so people can sit down and eat their donuts or have coffee. I'll have to clean those and make sure that the floor around them is swept too.

Uncle Charlie computerized the ordering systems last year, so all I'll have to do is just swipe what someone orders and it'll total it for me, keep track of the inventory, and even tell me how much change to give, which is good because Grandpa is a real stickler about that.

"A hundred pennies add up to a dollar!" he always yells when he finds random pennies on the floor or left on a table.

Dad will help me set up what we're calling my

"Dream Account," which is a bank account where I'll deposit my paycheck. I figure if I can save really well for six years, I can have a good portion to put toward my dream college.

So we're going to the bank. And of course my friend Lucy's mom works there. Because you can't go anywhere in this town without knowing someone.

"Well, hi, honey," she said. "Are you getting your own savings account? I'll bet you're saving all that summer money for new clothes!"

"Nope," said Dad. "This is college money."

"Oh, I see," she said, smiling. "In that case, let's make this official." She started typing information into the computer. "Okay. I have your address because I know it. . . ." She tapped the keyboard some more.

See what I mean? Everyone knows who I am and where I live. I wonder if people at the bank know how much money we have too.

After a few minutes, it was all set up. Afterward Dad showed me how to make a deposit and gave me my own bank card too.

I was so excited, not only because I had my own bank account, which felt very grown-up, but because the Dream Account was now crossed off my list, which meant I was that much closer to making my dream come true. I was almost hopping up and down in my seat in the car.

"You really want to get out of here, don't you?" asked Dad, and when he said it, it wasn't in his usual joking way. He sounded a little worried, and I immediately felt bad. It wasn't as if I just wanted to get away from Dad.

"You know," he said thoughtfully, "I get it."

"You do?" I asked.

"Yeah," he said. "I was the same way. I was itchy. I wanted to go see the big wide world."

We both stared ahead of us.

"I don't want to go to get away from you and Skylar," I said.

Dad nodded.

"But think of Wetsy Betsy."

Dad looked confused. "Who is Wetsy Betsy?"

"Wetsy Betsy is Elizabeth Ellis. In kindergarten she had an accident and wet her pants. And even now, like, seven years later, kids still call her Wetsy Betsy. It's like once you're known as something here, you can't shake it. You can't . . ." I trailed off.

"You can't reinvent yourself, you mean?" asked Dad.

"Exactly!" I said. "You are who you are and you can't ever change." I could tell Dad's mind was spinning.

"So who are you?" he asked after a few more minutes.

"What?" I asked.

"Who are you?" Dad asked. "If Elizabeth Ellis is Wetsy Betsy, then who are you?"

I took a deep breath. "I'm the girl whose mother died. I sometimes hear kids whisper about it when I walk by."

I saw Dad grimace. I looked out the window so I wouldn't have to watch him. We stayed quiet the rest of the way home.

We pulled up into our driveway and Dad turned off the car, but he didn't get out.

"I understand, honey. I really do. I understand dreaming. I understand getting away, starting fresh, starting over. But wherever you go, you take yourself with you, just remember that. You can start a new chapter and change things around, but sometimes you can't just rewrite the entire book," he said.

I thought about that. I didn't quite believe what he was saying, though. In school they were always nagging us about rewriting things.

"But you escaped," I said. "And then you just came back!"

"Well, you escape prison. I didn't see this place as a prison," Dad said. "But Nans as a warden, that's . . ." He started laughing. "Seriously, though, I left because I wanted an adventure. I wanted to meet new people and see if I could make it in a place where everyone didn't care about me and where I was truly on my own. I never had any plans to come back, but that's how it worked out."

"So why did you move back here?" I asked.

"Because of Mom," said Dad. "She loved this place. I brought her here to meet everyone and she didn't want to leave."

"But Mimi didn't want her to move here," I said, trying to piece together what happened.

I had always thought it was Dad who wanted to move back home. Mom and Dad met in college. She lived at school like Dad did, but Mimi was close by, so she could drive over for dinner. Mom and Dad hung out at Mimi's house a lot while they were in college.

"Noooo," Dad said slowly. "Mimi wasn't too thrilled about Mom's plan. She didn't really understand why Mom would want to move out here, so far from her family, and especially where there weren't a lot of opportunities for artists."

"So she changed her mind?" I asked.

I never remembered Mimi saying anything bad about where we lived, but Dad would always tease her, saying, "So it worked out okay, didn't it, Marla?"

She came to visit twice a year and always seemed to have a good time. "It's a beautiful place to live," she would say, smiling.

"Well," said Dad. "It took Mimi a while to change her mind. But she saw how happy Mom was and how much everyone here loved Mom, so she was happy that Mom was happy. That's the thing about parents. They really just want their kids to be happy, even if they don't understand why they do things. If you decide to move away from here, I'll miss you every day, but if that's what you want to do and that's what makes you happy, then I will be there with the moving truck."

"So if I tell you I want to move to Chicago for college, you'll be okay with that?" I asked.

"If you promise to come home and visit me a lot," said Dad, grinning.

"Deal!" I said.

"I love you," said Dad.

"I love you back," I said.

"Okay, kiddo, let's go in for dinner. Nans goes mad when we're late."

"Dad, isn't it correct to say that Nans gets angry? Because, like, animals go mad but people get angry."

"In that definition, Lindsay, I think that is an entirely correct way to categorize your grandmother when you are late for dinner. She gets mad!"

I giggled and opened the car door.

"Ready, set, run to the warden!" said Dad, and we raced up to the house, bursting with laughter.

First Day of Work

The plan was that I'd start working at Donut Dreams two weeks before school started. That way I'd get into my regular routine and not have to adjust to a job at the Park and a new school at the same time. For the school year, I'll work after school two days a week and one day on the weekends.

But since much of the waitstaff take vacations at the end of the summer, it was all hands on deck, according to Grandpa, and the whole family was taking full-day shifts at the restaurant.

Mornings were always way complicated because things start early in the restaurant business. Even if the Park didn't open until six thirty in the morning, that meant everyone, including the cooks, the busboys, and the waitresses, got there by five o'clock to start prepping the food, brewing coffee, sorting the daily bread deliveries, and making sure the ovens were on.

Since we own Donut Dreams, everyone just assumes that we eat donuts at every meal, and that they're stacked everywhere in our house. But we actually eat like everyone else, and Nans only lets us have donuts on the weekends, just like Mom did.

So Monday morning I put on my Dream Team T-shirt and got downstairs early. Nans already had my fruit and juice at my place at the table. Since she got up early to make the donuts, by the time Skylar and I got up, she joked that she should be making lunch. Dad had to be at the restaurant early in the morning, so after Mom died, Nans was the one who came back home from the restaurant to stay with us when Dad had to leave.

Nans was making me scrambled eggs and I was surprised to see Skylar, still in his pj's, eating his cereal.

"What are you doing up?" I asked. "It's not like you have to go to work today."

"Nans woke me up," he whined. "We have to drive you to work. So even if I don't have to go to work, I still have to get up."

"You can get in the car in your pajamas!" Nans said, exasperated. "I just can't leave you here alone while I run Lindsay to work!"

Skylar rolled his eyes. "Well, can I at least get a donut while we're there?"

Nans sighed. "Sure," she said with a grin. "On Saturday."

It probably seems weird to eat breakfast before you go to work in a restaurant, but working in a restaurant is hard, and you don't get a lot of breaks. It's not like you can stuff snacks in your apron pockets either. You're on your feet the whole time and running around, and you can barely sip a drink, let alone eat. During slow times the staff will grab a plate in the kitchen, but as soon as you have a customer you have to put it down, so no one ever has a leisurely burger or anything.

Nans jingled her keys, and Skylar sighed loudly and pushed back his chair. I took one last look in the mirror before we left, and then Nans drove down the curvy road toward the restaurant.

I could ride my bike to work, especially in nice weather, but Mom would never, ever let us ride on Park Street. She said people went too fast around the curves.

It's kind of weird that even though Mom died, some of her rules are still here, and nobody has tried to get rid of them. At first we did things like staying up really late because everyone was so distracted, and nobody seemed to notice. Plus, there were, like, hundreds of people at the house and stopping in at all hours.

But one night at dinner, Dad said, "Okay, life as we know it is going to be very different, but there are ground rules that stay the same."

After that we had bedtimes and regular meals and all the old rules seemed to kick back in.

When we pulled up to the restaurant, it was six fifteen. You could tell Nans was torn, because she wanted to go in and check things out and get a few things done in the office, but Sky was scowling.

Nans glanced in the back seat. "Sky, do you want to go say hi to your dad?"

But before he could answer, Dad came bounding out of the restaurant. "A fine family morning!" he bellowed, smiling at me. "Look at this wonderful employee on her first day at Donut Dreams!"

He actually looked really proud, and I kind of blushed a little.

"She's going to be spectacular, as always!" said Nans, smiling.

"And I get to see my boy!" said Dad, reaching in to give Sky a squeeze.

"I had to get up early," Skylar whined.

"Good practice for when school starts!" said Dad. "And since you made the very big effort of getting into the car, I have a little treat for you." He handed Skylar a bag.

"Donuts!" screamed Skylar, and Dad laughed.

"First-day-of-work exception," Dad said. "Don't get too used to it!" He gave Skylar a kiss on the head and added, "Have fun at camp!"

Then he turned to me and opened the car door. "And you, my dear, are mine for the day. Let's get to work!"

My cousin Kelsey was also working behind the counter at Dreams, and she gave me a quick wave when I came in.

Kelsey and my other four cousins all work at the Park and Dreams. Kelsey is only older than me by a month and a half, but she always tells people I'm her younger cousin.

"You know what to do?" asked Kelsey.

I nodded and slipped behind the counter with her and put on an apron. Dad was talking to the manager of the restaurant about something, so I turned around and stared at the rows of donuts, making sure they were all lined up and that the shelves were clean.

When Mom was alive I went home right after school, but after she died, Dad would pick Skylar and me up and bring us to the restaurant so we could be near him. We'd hang out at a table and do our homework or color for a few hours before Nans would take us home for dinner. I had watched the counter at Dreams for a few years, so now I knew exactly what had to be done.

If you look around, a restaurant is kind of a fascinating place. It's usually busy—if it's a good restaurant, that is—and there are people sitting and talking about stuff, and if you pay attention, you can learn a lot. And most people don't stop talking when someone comes over to the table. So even if I helped clear a table or dropped off a glass of water, I could really get an earful. That's what I loved most, picking up little pieces about people that you wouldn't normally know.

Grandpa loves to go around and talk to everyone,

and he stops and chats with the regulars, especially the ones at the counter in the morning. He knows everything that was going on in town, but he never spilles it to any of us, which drove Mom crazy.

"Oh, come on," she'd say. "I know they were probably talking about it at the Park. What's the dirt?"

And he would just smile and shake his head and say, "I just pour the coffee. What do I know?"

But Grandpa never misses a beat, so you have to be on your toes. I once saw him correct people for not properly wiping down a table, or not setting it right, or sloshing a glass of water when they put it down.

I know that he likes things tidy, which is hard when you sell donuts, because some of them have sprinkles or are crumbly. So when you lift them off the tray, you get crumbs everywhere—on the shelf, on the floor, and sometimes on the counter.

At Dreams there's a lot of wiping and sweeping, because if Grandpa sees sprinkles all over the glass counter, he won't be pleased. He'll say, "Is that counter eating those sprinkles?" So the first thing I did was wipe down the counter, which was already clean.

"Ugh," whispered Kelsey, "it's the East twins."

The East twins were running up to the case and

putting their fingers all over the glass front. The two boys were adorable, but every time they came in, they made a huge mess.

"Hi, Mrs. East," said Kelsey. "What can we get you today?"

Mrs. East always looked like she'd just run through a windstorm. There were always papers coming out of her bag, and her clothes were usually wrinkled or stained.

But she was really nice, and after Mom died she made us a lot of dinners and brought them over. She even came over with a picnic lunch one day for me and Sky and took us to the park.

"Oh, let me get the boys settled here," she said, lifting them into chairs. "Jason, please stop hitting your brother!"

"That one, that one!" the boys started yelling, waving their little hands at the donuts.

"Boys!" said Mrs. East. "Use your manners! And Christopher, stop screaming!"

The boys scrambled off their chairs and ran back to the counter. Luckily, there was no one else waiting, because it took them a full ten minutes to choose their donuts.

I had one hand over the chocolate iced one when Christopher yelled, "No, no, no, not that one!" and I had to move my hand around the shelf until it was hovering over the "right" one.

"Thank you," said Mrs. East. "You girls are amazingly patient! And I'm more frazzled today than usual. We just got back from vacation with my mom, and even though we love them, moms can be such a pain sometimes. Right, girls?"

She looked up as she was handing us the money for the donuts and froze. Her eyes went wide as she looked at me, remembering, and then her hand flew over her mouth.

Kelsey shifted from foot to foot nervously.

This happens a lot. People will say things and then be really scared that they said the wrong thing in front of you. Before Mom died, even when she was sick, all of a sudden everyone was really careful about what they said around me. For a month after Mom died, my friends wouldn't even talk about their moms in front of me.

I talked to Aunt Melissa about it, because she was who I went to for a lot of stuff these days.

"Honey, people are trying to be considerate. But

sometimes you have to help them, too," Aunt Melissa told me.

Poor Mrs. East looked a little like she might cry. Kelsey looked at me expectantly.

"Yeah, you should hear Kelsey complain about Aunt Melissa," I joked.

Kelsey opened the cash drawer and smiled. "Yeah, but she's got nothing on Nans, and you basically live with Nans."

We laughed, but Mrs. East still stood there, silent. I could tell she still felt awful.

"That'll be five fifty, please," said Kelsey, and Mrs. East suddenly looked down and realized she still had the donut money in her hand.

"Oh thank you, honey," she said.

She took the donuts to the boys, who shoved them into their mouths in five seconds flat. Then she walked back over and grabbed some extra napkins.

"Sometimes you take things for granted," she said to me, I guess as an apology. "How was your summer, Lindsay? You excited for your first day at Bellgrove Middle School? Oh and the big Fall Fling is soon, right? Did you do any dress shopping this summer?"

Fall Fling is, I guess, a big deal. It's the fall dance at

the middle school, and everybody goes. I think they go because there's not much else to do, but kids start talking about it around the Fourth of July.

My BFF, Casey, had already started looking online for a dress, and she's been poking me to go shopping. The thing is that shopping for school is a little weird these days. Usually Aunt Melissa takes me and Kelsey to the mall that's an hour and a half away and we stock up, or we just order stuff online.

"I'm not ready to start thinking about school," I said. "It's still summer!"

"You're right!" laughed Mrs. East. "You enjoy every last drop of summer!"

Then she went over to try to wipe the boys' faces, which were covered in donut icing. It was also in their hair.

"So did you pick out a dress yet?" I asked Kelsey.

"Not yet," she said. "I found a few online that Mom said she'd order so I can try them on. Here, I'll show you."

She grabbed her phone from behind the counter, which was a big no-no. Grandpa did not let anyone have a phone when they were "on the floor," which meant out in the open in the restaurant.

Looking for another great book?
Find it
IN THE MIDDLE.

Fun, fantastic books for kids
in the in-be**TWEEN** age.

IntheMiddleBooks.com

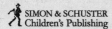 

Still Hungry?

There's always room for

a Cupcake!

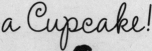

Katie and the cupcake cure

Mia in the mix

Emma on thin icing

Alexis and the perfect recipe

Katie, batter up!

Mia's baker's dozen

CUPCAKE DIARIES

Emma all stirred up!
by coco simon

CUPCAKE DIARIES

Alexis cool as a cupcake
by coco simon

CUPCAKE DIARIES

Katie and the cupcake war

CUPCAKE DIARIES

Mia's boiling point

CUPCAKE DIARIES

Emma, smile and say "cupcake!"

CUPCAKE DIARIES

Alexis gets frosted

CUPCAKE DIARIES

Katie's new recipe

CUPCAKE DIARIES

Mia a matter of taste

CUPCAKE DIARIES

Emma sugar + spice and everything nice

CUPCAKE DIARIES

Alexis and the missing ingredient
by coco simon

CUPCAKE DIARIES

Katie sprinkles & surprises

CUPCAKE DIARIES

Mia fashion plates and cupcakes

sew Zoey

Zoey's clothing design blog puts her on the A-list in the fashion world . . . but when it comes to school, will she be teased, or will she be a trendsetter? Find out in the Sew Zoey series: